Unconditional Surrender

Also by Emyr Humphreys
from seren

A Toy Epic
Outside the House of Baal

Unconditional Surrender

EMYR HUMPHREYS

seren

seren is the book imprint of
Poetry Wales Press Ltd
Wyndham Street, Bridgend, Wales

© Emyr Humphreys, 1996

The right of Emyr Humphreys to be identified as the Author
of this Work has been asserted in accordance with the
Copyright, Designs and Patents Act, 1988.

First published in hardback 1996
paperback edition 1997

A British Library Cataloguing in Publication record
for this title is available from the CIP Office

ISBN 1-85411-213-9

Published with the financial support of
the Arts Council of Wales

Printed in Plantin by
Creative Print and Design, Ebbw Vale

The two voices of this novel belong to the former Countess Cecilia von Leiden and the Reverend Edwin Pritchard, the Rector of the Parish of Garth Llanfair in the County of Caernarfon. They speak in turn between May and August in the summer of 1945.

ONE

i

'From now on,' the girl said. 'Every day will be an opportunity for doing good.' My throat was dry with the desire to tell her how much I loved her. I knew my smile looked fixed and forced. She was the heaven-sent messenger of peace, my Meg, not yet eighteen, glowing with health, her cold hands clutching the handle-bars of her precious bicycle.

'That's the real meaning to unconditional surrender,' she said. 'When you come to think about it. The absolutely fresh start. Why shouldn't we build a better world? Why shouldn't we?'

What could I do except agree with her impossible ambition. The war was over and she was leaning towards me over her bicycle ready to take on the world. The sunlight was an aura around her lovely head. There is nothing I would not do for her. It was for this we were created after all. She glides through the magical transformations of early May knowing how to renew everything. She brings revelations. I have to restrain myself from gripping her arms and never letting her go. I must keep my sense of proportion. She has only called in order to reassure her mother that I am alright. Her eager beauty makes me want to weep. She has so much to do. So many to attend to. I must not become an encumbrance, a purposeless deadweight.

'I must go, Countess.'

She has letters to post for her father. The most important to her brother serving in North Africa. I cannot hold her back any longer. On either side of the overgrown drive to this Residential Home for Decayed Gentlewomen the trees are ready to part so that she can ride unimpeded towards the wilderness of this world. She leaves me here leaning on my stick. The longer you live the more vulnerable you become. At fifty-seven I am as stiff as a figure in a wooden clock. Carved to mark out arthritic time.

She leaves me and a cloud passes over the sun. I am marooned again in my own harsh reality. I know so little it is worse than knowing nothing. A refugee in a foreign land. There is nothing wrong with the Refuge. I would carry the misery in me wherever I went, just as the days are bound to go by and the war was bound to end.

It's all over and it is not over. How can it be when catastrophe recurs night after night in my dreams. Whatever life is left can only be kept going by a steady transfusion of goodwill and affection. I must bind her to me. I can never let her go. And yet if my grip is too tight she will struggle to escape. Who would want to waste affection on a crumbling old hag like me? The girl and her mother give me tolerance and kindness and that should be enough. But I crave for affection. I am trapped in this institution like a moulting bird in an iron cage. In my little rooms I am surrounded by dead souvenirs and mementoes and objects drained of whatever significance they once possessed. They are further evidence of my obsolescence and yet I cannot summon up the strength to throw them away. I have to go on believing in their value. The only vital force in those corridors is the unrelenting hostility of a monstrous regiment of old women. And I am supposed to be grateful for a roof over my head. Non-combatants indeed. They are armed to their false teeth with venom.

Decayed gentlewomen indeed. They are pulsating with aggression. They will have me apologize daily for my mere existence. On my way out I encountered the asthmatic Letitia Hughes-White in the corridor and she summoned up her strength to hiss at me 'We've won. We've won the war. Nothing to stop you going home now, Countess. Won't that be nice?' She delivered her thrust and did not wait for a response. As she moved away I could hear her muttering to herself, 'If she is a Countess. If it matters anyway. Germany is finished.' She shone so full of triumph, her twisted form seemed to illuminate the gloom of the corridor.

Did I lock my door? I was so eager to get out into the sunlight. These elementary precautions I can never get used to. Three weeks ago Wayne and Sandra the caretaker's brats had the top off my portable Imperial typewriter to play with the keys. Before that I caught their older brother Denzil on his knees in front of the cupboard at the bottom of the so-called chiffonier in my bedroom. They were locked, but he wouldn't need all that much strength to open them. Things are so easily stolen. One should never forget that. And that is where I store my treasure. I was in too much pain and confusion at the time to cross-examine the boy. He had an excuse. The caretaker's children always have excuses. I barely heard it. My mind was throbbing with recollections of Gottfried. He was such a perfect dancer. In his uniform he was as immaculate as an oil painting. When I was seventeen I longed for him to kiss me. Our ways had long since parted. And yet in those moments we were as close as dancers. The only alternative to shooting someone else is shooting yourself. It seems obvious, and yet when it happens it comes as a paralysing surprise. Was it out of shame he shot himself? Make it all un-happen. Liquidate an intolerable history. Obliterate a world.

Meg is right. The fresh start. A new world. What's left of me and mine should be directed to helping her. She shall have my treasure. To do with it as she thinks fit. If it is still there. I am seized with a sudden panic. I had to get back as quickly as I could and check the contents. Jewels. You can't eat them. Icons I no longer worship. Except for the jewelled cross that was made for a von Leiden in fifteenth century Nürnberg. Everything I could save and keep close to me, she should have them. At the very least they should be in a safer place.

ii

What am I to do with her? My committee recommends that she be repatriated as soon as possible. So easy for them to talk. *The Rector will see to it.* Those patronising smiles across the table declare that it is what I am paid to do. It goes with the job. By the terms of the Bequest the incumbent administers and remains responsible to the Committee of Management. *It is true we suspended the constitutional rules for the Duration...* our legal expert licks his lips... *but the terms of our Endowment specifically define 'Decayed Gentlewomen' as 'Spinsters of gentle birth native to any of the six counties of North Wales'.* It couldn't be clearer. The Countess has been married twice, and if she is to be believed, was born in Schleswig Holstein.

What am I to do with her? My wife and daughter were quick to find a loophole. That word *duration*. The war is not over. Except in Europe. My Olwen and my Meg argue the woman should be left in peace as long as possible. I concur as long as my peace is included in the pattern. It has to be admitted the woman is a disruptive force and my committee would like to see her removed in one way or another. Olwen and Meg point out it would be impractical and inhuman to send her back. And where do I stand? The fact is when we take a hand in the fate of others we call our own existence into question.

Now where is that girl off to? I tap the study window with my ruler.

'Meg! Come here a minute, would you?'

Half the time I have no idea where she's off to. I don't know whether it's the end of the war in Europe but she flies about on that bicycle of hers as if it were her mission in life to proclaim the birth of freedom. The girl has work to do. Exams to pass. Freedom doesn't mean you are perpetually making your escape. It is too late to open the window and bawl after her. In any case the window is stuck. It hasn't been painted for five years.

And I have duties of my own to attend to. I sit at my desk in the bay window with a sermon to begin let alone finish. *And God said, let us make man in our image after our likeness: and let him have dominion over the fish in the sea, and over the fowl of the air, and over the cattle, and over all the earth....* The war in Europe is over, and this green landscape I stare at through the bay window knows nothing about it. What am I supposed to be celebrating? The bovine indifference of nature? In the Bible the trees rejoice and the mountains and the valleys clap their hands. My business should be to advertise the way to a better world. And here I sit just as unmoved as the gorse that blooms on the hill: condemned for life to rewriting the first paragraph of a sermon, *And God said, let us make man in our image after our likeness*.... Ingenious ants crawl over the planet organised for slaughter, unable to distinguish between the song of triumph and the dance of death. With our own hands we open a concentration camp like a tin of worms and there's no sign of God's image inside. Only the Devil's.

I long to be cheerful. As cheerful as my wife. Olwen is endowed with good nature and she has a faith far superior to mine. She must have. Otherwise how can she sing as she goes about her laborious chores in an ill-lit old-fashioned rectory kitchen? Most days in one way or another she tells me to cheer up and stop brooding.

Now that the hostilities in Europe are ended our son should be safe. We have a clever healthy daughter. Olwen points out how much we have to be grateful for. In a world drenched with suffering we have been allowed not to suffer. Go and write your sermon, she says. My fountain pen circles over the space where a word should be and refuses to appear. I look up and the problem transforms into a displaced person.

Here she comes. She has already spotted me. Certain individuals are sent to test the limits of our patience. The Countess Cecilia von Leiden. I restrain my pen from writing down her name in the empty space on my pad. Alias Mrs Clarke. This one on any day of the week for the last five years has been endowed with the gift of becoming the bane of my existence. And yet my wife encourages her. My daughter I sometimes think dotes on her. Which puts me at a permanent disadvantage. Here she comes. I square my shoulders to confront frankness with frankness. I will not allow my natural affability to give the impression of ingratiating obsequiousness. Is there any hope she will turn left and make straight for the kitchen? In that case I could reschedule my day and start visiting while she regales my Olwen with yet another instalment of aristocratic reminiscence. That amuses me. Olwen still calls herself a Christian Socialist. She claims to be immune to any Anglican inclination towards titles and snobbery and attributes this to her rugged nonconformist origins. She laughed at my pleasure at being invited to Lord Devonal's country house for a seminar on post-war ecclesiastical policy. And yet it is she with all her Left Book leanings who has enticed this displaced aristocrat into our home. In the thirties she used to encourage me to preach social justice and pacifism with outspoken zeal. The bishop did not approve. It did harm to my chances of preferment. These days I keep my thoughts more to myself. When I woke up this morning I concluded the price of victory will be indistinguishable from the price of defeat: unrationed guilt all around and a sliding scale of enslavement, depravation, hunger. And so I struggle to compose homilies on civilised decencies and the wellsprings of good behaviour.

She is crossing the lawn and is advancing towards me with teutonic resolution. She will get her feet wet. I should have mown the lawn yesterday afternoon. Olwen says I need more exercise. Goodness knows what the woman is carrying in that basket on her arm: some book in gothic script she thinks our Meg should read; a cake made from a pungent central European recipe; the programme of some concert she happened to attend when Richard Strauss himself no less was conducting; any trifle that will allow her to adopt a bountiful air and avoid the role of indigent supplicant. The nearer she approaches the stronger the current of uncharitable thoughts I am obliged to subdue. She is smiling her long-toothed smile as though the pleasantry with which she will greet me when I open the side door is already forming in her mind. Solitary persons have ample time to rehearse their speeches.

'Ah dear Mr Pritchard. You are the most fortunate among men.'

'Why do you say that, Countess?'

Olwen insists we address her as 'Countess'. 'Why not Mrs Clarke?' I say. 'She needs it. She needs all the encouragement she can get in her circumstances.' She crosses the threshold of my refuge like the advance guard of an occupying power. Her walking stick and even her basket are potential offensive weapons.

She sits and she is holding court among my bookshelves.

'You may not be rich in cattle, but you have everything else.'

She felt that I was slow to understand.

'Admetus,' she said.

She looked around my books in a way that suggested I should open them more often.

'You are protected by the gods,' she said.

As always her accented oracular delivery made me uneasy. She delivered all her pronouncements with a superior benevolence. And those teeth suggested she found me a source of unfailing amusement. Why come to me and not go straight to the kitchen?

'You possess the pearl above price, Rector.'

This time I restrained myself from asking. She stared at me as she prepared to share her secret.

'Inner peace. I think that is what you are hiding.'

iii

It wasn't at all what I meant to say to him. All I had in mind was a simple question — 'Ah my dear man of the cloth, what shall we do with the Dead?' But what could he tell me? And what right have I to demand an answer? This is Maytime. As I passed near the wood I heard birdsong. I was surrounded by green leaves and white blossom as though a sequence of weddings were in progress between the flowered earth and the blue sky. Yet I could not rejoice. There was so much distress festering inside me. By what angelic edict had this corner of the world been exempt from the rampage of evil? What could he tell me? The third son of a hill farmer turned to the established church in the hope of a more cloistered existence. So his wife told me with that forgiving smile I cherish and covet. 'Dear Edwin,' she says. 'He might as well be a poet, he is so sensitive. He has one layer of skin less than the rest of us. Perhaps he is a poet. Or let's say an historian who yearns to sing the praises of the distant past. Do you know what I mean?' I could listen to her for hours on end. Not so much for what she says as for the music in her voice. I love the warmth of her speech as she plies the mysteries of her craft around her kitchen. She can prepare excellent food out of the most unlikely ingredients. That makes a palpable link between her labours and the nature of existence. But what is he doing? I listen to his sermons when they are in English and try as I will I find little in them other than homiletic bromides. Not that I would ever breathe a word of such a subversive opinion. We are outside salvation if there is no one to save us.

'The news, Rector. I can no longer take it in. My mind rejects it. I can't digest it. I have to admit to being a product of a murderous jungle. How can I?'

I am giving him a chance to speak. He can hear me but he says nothing. He sits in his mahogany desk-chair and stares at me like a lugubrious owl. He says such vapid things. Last Sunday, for example, in a damp aside welcoming the prospect of a general election in the United Kingdom: *The chief purpose, let us not forget, of making changes in the social order should be to give individuals wider opportunities of refining their own natures....* This could well be true but he turned it into a platitudinous pancake. And who am I to judge. His wife approves. Across the aisle I saw the faint smile on her face as he said it.

'What are we to think, Rector? The fruits of two thousand years of Christianity are the camps and the gas-ovens?'

I only wanted him to catch a glimpse of the depth of my pain.

'The civilisation of Germany, Countess, to be precise.'

It was enough to show how much he disliked me. A brief flash of light in the murk. I had to brace myself. I had a position to defend. But not so vigorously as to lose my foothold in this house. It was the last refuge left to me in this world. I had to smile and reassure. I had to display controlled sophistication.

'The world will change so rapidly now, Rector. We shall soon be obsolete, you and I. I wonder what we can do about it?'

'Very little, I'm afraid.'

'If there is a future it belongs to Meg. It is Meg we should be thinking about. When you love someone she becomes precious,

Mr Pritchard, and when they become precious they need to be protected.'

I could see him stiffen in his seat. It was no part of my business to be overly concerned for his daughter. I was an intruder threatening the inner sanctum of his patriarchal domain. But there could be no turning back. All I could do was humble my pride and press on with my mission.

'I love Meg, Mr Pritchard. Your dear wife knows how much I love her. A beautiful young girl is such a precious thing. I have no right. She is not mine. She is yours. And then again she is not yours. She is herself and she will always have a duty to herself. Our affections can lead us into such confusion. In any case I want to help. I want to be allowed to help.'

I lifted the basket like a peasant in the market place unused to trading and over-anxious to display her wares. Jewels are like a fantasy. Rings and bracelets and necklaces. Gold. Amethyst. Sapphire. Ruby. Diamond. The wondrous cross. As much as escaped Tom Clarke's avaricious thieving fingers. The cross and the icons he was afraid of. He thought they were loaded with centuries of ill luck.

'Why wait until I am dead? That's what I think dear Mr Pritchard. "For a short time a woman is fair and that is her hour of danger". Do you know the saying? It may be a new world coming but that kind of wisdom doesn't change, Rector. I ask you to allow me to help her. As I long to. Since you are her father. So that she can pursue a career of her own choosing. Enjoy an independence that will last her for life. I make my will in her favour of course, but why wait? Why deny myself the pleasure of handing her what could ensure her independence and her freedom.... You object?'

I was too vehement. I knew it. My eyes watered and the shape in his chair began to shrink with the effort of increasing the distance between us. I had to stop. The more effort I made towards understanding and a true meeting of minds the further he shrank away from me.

'It is not a question of objecting, Countess. I could not possibly allow.... I recognise your generosity of course but I could not possibly allow Meg to accept.... I recognise your goodwill of course, but these jewels....'

'They are mine,' I said. 'I assure you.'

He did not smile. Our Rector has very little sense of humour.

'I don't doubt it. I don't doubt it for one moment. You put me in a difficult position....'

He looked so confused and embarrassed. I tried to spare him.

'It is easier to give than to accept. That has always been my experience. In any case I am begging. We can talk about Meg again. What I ask now is to leave my little treasure in your safe. Under lock and key. I ask this great favour.'

I smile as winningly as I know how. I was never a great beauty. My Nanny brushed my hair into curls with rosewater so that I could be presented to my parents and their guests at tea-time. I believed them when they said how pretty I was. On the threshold of adolescence a nasty cousin called me 'horse-face'. I lost hours of sleep when I overheard my mother worrying about the size of my nose. She couldn't bear to look at me until I got engaged and everything was settled and approved of and I was to become the Countess von Leiden. Manfred was handsome. The wedding was spectacular enough. My mother never learnt he preferred men to women. Those far-off days, and here am I still smiling my horsey smile and waiting for approval.

iv

Whether the jewels are genuine or not, the woman's purpose is clear enough. She wants to put me permanently in her debt. Her generous gesture is a direct attack on the integrity and autonomy of my family. She looks at me with her hungry smile and she has no inkling of the damage she is inflicting on my nerves. The inviolability of my family means everything to me. This German woman has no conception of the strains and stresses inherent in my cultural background. My brother Henry stayed at home on the hill farm so that I could go to university and to Oxford. I am obliged to sit here and listen to her ponderous accent, but what I hear is my mother whispering as she lies in bed dying of cancer. A small lamp burns in the corner of her bedroom. She clutches my arm with her thin hand. I am hearing the strains of our sad music for the last time. Muted strings. *'Cofia Edwin... Remember Edwin we never go asking for favours. We have always sacrificed everything for each other....'* The family pride of hill farmers. The hard-won independence and self-reliance. The thought brings tears to my eyes. So humble and so proud. How can this foreign aristocrat understand? Every vacation I slaved on the farm from morning till night in a desperate effort to ease my brother's burden as much as I could. What else kept us going except family pride and a determination to be in no one's debt? This foreign creature could hardly be expected to understand that.

'I can never go back, Rector, you see. Never.'

Now what is she talking about? Every time she opens her mouth she unsettles me. She sits in my study as though by divine right, and conducts a conversation that takes for granted that I take a keen interest in her welfare.

'In fact there is nowhere I can go back to. The Russians have kindly occupied what was left of my husband's estate. And to the best of my knowledge, which as you know is painfully limited, our people have fled to the West.'

The woman suffers from grandiose illusions. 'Our people' indeed. Counting their serfs as souls. That sort of thing. If ever a revolution was overdue. Her presence is the incarnation of an unacceptable past. She is history giving me a headache.

'Not that they would want to see me again in any case. I have the word "traitor" branded on my forehead. I have spent the war hiding on the wrong side.'

Her teeth give the impression that she is still smiling. I have to tell her with as much tact as I can muster that she needs her jewels herself to survive in a hostile world. Sooner or later she will have to be moved out of the Residence for Decayed Gentlewomen. And then where would she go? I can foresee a tide of uncomfortable crises that will culminate in this formidable female taking up residence in this very house. She already sits in front of me preening her feathers: an objectionable cuckoo in my nest.

'I know some of those silly old women are longing to get rid of me. But I can never go back. And quite frankly I don't want to.'

Putting the jewels away in a safe gives me an opportunity to turn my back on the Countess. The safe was presented to my predecessor when the part-time branch of the Gwynedd Farmers' Bank in the lower village was closed. A comforting solid piece of local history. To get at it I have to move my golf clubs rusting away in their leather bag. When will I ever play again? Olwen makes fun of the attachment I have to objects with which I surround myself for comfort and protection. Those rows of pipes. Those college photographs and wooden crests. The dictionaries of languages I no longer study. The boxes of books and papers I have accumulated in preparation for my exhaustive history of the parish. I touch them daily with my toecap and cherish their talismanic power. It will be my contribution to the sum of human understanding: a definitive history of the parish from the day it took shape, four thousand, six hundred million years ago to the hour I sit down to write. A matter of depth rather than breadth. With my name on it.

'You will think it none of my business, Rector, but I have so much regard for Meg. I have to say this. This Griff person. Our conscientious objector. He may be a scientific genius, I would not know. In any case, he is not good enough for her. He is weak. He depends too much on her strength. She is so young and the young are so liable to be misled by some brand or other of idealism.'

I maintain a silence in the hope that she will realise that these are matters I have no wish to discuss with her. In any case we have been over the business of what she calls idealism, so many times before. When she digs those teeth into an argument she won't let go. It's more than a question of style. My wife and my daughter talk of the positive structure of North German speech to excuse the irritation of her uncompromising imperatives.

What can I say in reply except '*Judge not that ye be not judged*'. Or something much sharper. It was time for me to summon up the strength of character, the courage, should I call it, to draw her attention to the letter of complaints against her, addressed to my committee and signed by all but two of the inmates of the Residence. The shining exceptions as always are the twins, Flora Elizabeth and Clarice May, aged eighty-four, who peer at the world out of a cocoon of euphoric deafness and understand very little except each other and the rubrics of practised piety.

'Countess. There is a matter to which I have to draw your attention....'

I lock the safe and replace the key in the top right-hand drawer of the roll-top desk. I am too slow. Like a person forewarned she is already on her feet. She grips her stick as though she exercised the authority to bring an interview to an end.

'My dear Rector, I am so relieved. My jewels were in never better keeping. Under lock and key. In your safe. In your study. Now with your permission I shall go and pay my respects to your dear wife.'

I was so relieved to be rid of her I went along with the pretence that she had not heard me speak of a matter to which I had to draw her attention.

In the doorway she weighed heavily on her stick in order to turn and award me a parting smile. 'The war may be over, Rector, but I think we are all still prisoners in one way or another.'

TWO

i

It was kind of him to stop. In order to fill my lungs with the sea air and to hear the skylarks singing over the marsh, I had ventured too far along the foreshore and my back was hurting.

'Good afternoon, Countess. Can I offer you a lift?'

A displaced person whose vision is clouded with pain needs to be more than grateful. I smiled at him as flatteringly as I knew how and his black moustache spread above his mouth as he gripped the steering wheel of his jeep with gloved hands. He was a good-looking man and he was dedicated to playing the role of officer and gentleman. Uniforms have a way of transforming commonplace fellows into gallant knights.

'You are extremely kind, Colonel Bacon.'

He leapt down to help an arthritic old creature into the awkward passenger seat. So perfectly groomed. A faint smell of aftershave lotion about his person. The white hair at his temples in tasteful contrast with his black eyebrows, brushed and polished as thoroughly as his Sam Browne belt. And what is this human red-haired bundle on the back seat, with his knees at the side of his chin, and his pale blue eyes looking straight through me fixed on some blurred mark in his own memory? A tame Prisoner-of-War, disarmed and harmless as a domestic animal.

'You'll never guess where we're off to,' Colonel Bacon said.

He was naturally cheerful. As ebullient and free of inhibitions as only an Englishman can be. What was he in civil life? Olwen had told me. Manager of a small town branch of the Halifax Building Society. And here he was conducting himself like a General in the vanguard of a victorious army.

'We are going to chapel,' he said.

Everything was so amusing. Well at least it was a cheerful attitude.

'Believe it or not I've got a genius there trapped on the back seat. Klaus Wilhelm Rist. K.W.R. I call him for short. It's up to me to see that he practises, what?'

I recognised the Colonel was affecting what he took to be a carefree upper-class English manner. There was no harm in it. In my straightened circumstances there was a certain amount of pleasure to be derived from observing the social mores of another country. It was less strenuous than birdwatching. He was in command of the Prisoner-of-War camp. Those dismal huts on the wasteland near the estuary. Those human cages. I encounter him in the Rectory which he has taken to haunt almost as much as I do. Olwen is the attraction. She is amused by his elegant manner and his trick of bending his knees like a tentative invitation to dance. She accepts his gifts of sugar and margarine and warns Meg and me to say nothing to the Rector about it. Little kitchen subterfuges. Meg smothers her disapproval and when she gets the chance engages the Colonel in impudent political argument. I adore the Rectory kitchen and such encounters that send shafts of warmth and light into my bleak existence.

'I believe in keeping my captives usefully employed as far as rules allow,' the Colonel said. 'But we can't have K.W.R. ruin his hands digging ditches, can we?'

This was amusing too. The chapel dominated the village. Hideous façade. A democratic cathedral I have been assured, built with their own hands. That sort of thing. 'The Mosque' Olwen called it. It was Calvinistic Methodist. And since she had been brought up a Baptist, as she explained to me, she felt no particular reverence towards it. But it boasted the biggest and the best organ in the district.

Here, Olwen said, the majority pursued their awkward and unaesthetic devotions, dominated by pulpit eloquence and emotional congregational singing. A synagogue, I said, more than a mosque. It has struck me before the Welsh are like the Jews. Maybe, Olwen said, but without any business sense. The Rectory kitchen has a pleasant tendency to echo our laughter.

Delicately I asked the Colonel if I could sit at the back of the chapel and listen. I think I made apparent my hope that the music would transport me to a more congenial level of existence, even evoke the glories of my past and disclose through the present cloud a vision of a better future.

At first the sheer volume of discordant staccato blasts unsettled my nerves to the extent of making me want to shout out. The Prisoner-of-War was crouched over the keyboard like a monster in an expressionist film from the twenties. Perhaps that was his intention. The yellow circle on his back was presumably a target for one of the armed guards to shoot at should the prisoner take it into his mind to run. I could shout at it instead of shooting. The colonel had sensed my discomfort. He climbed the red carpet of the pulpit steps to reach out and tap the organist on the back. After the silence and the echoing whispers I was given a soothing composition that might have been Bach or an improvisation of his own. How rapidly music can alter a mood. Now I was very ready to sing his praises. It occurred to me I should invite them both to tea at the Residence. It was cramped and overcrowded but surely an improvement on the huts in the prison camp. And their visit would be noticed by the inmates. My prestige would be enhanced by entertaining a British officer, so obviously an English gentleman: and if he had a prisoner in tow, invisible chains would be there to embellish a triumphant entry.

The Colonel approached me, tapping his fingertips along the surfaces of the pew-backs. I must have been smiling. The music filled the emptiness of the interior more pleasingly than the smell of polish.

'My dear Countess, I have a few things I have to attend to.'

Are his eyes rolling or has he brought his pink face too close to mine?

'Would you be so kind as to keep an eye on the prisoner, for half an hour or so? He's quite harmless. He speaks perfect English....'

He twiddled a gloved finger to underline the humour of it.

'But my goodness so do you! I shan't mind at all if you decide to chat away in German while I'm out. If I'm out I won't feel left out....'

He was laughing as he left me. To the victor the world has to be a jolly place. He can afford to be magnanimous. I was being given a concert all to myself. The sun came out and shone through the long windows to transform the austere chapel into a musical palace of dreams. The pews built for rows of pious peasants were all empty so that ghosts could take their ease and my youth like Eurydice return from the dead through the power of music. I closed my eyes and tried to live in the past. When I opened them the prisoner stood in the aisle in front of me. He was staring at me as if I were an unidentified object retrieved from an excavated tomb. I had to make my impression and I was so pleased when the lines of a poem came to my mind.

'"Und die Musik, immer neu, aus den bebendsten Steinen..." and so on. You play very well, young man.'

'Speak English,' he said.

He spoke quietly enough but I resented being ordered what language to speak. I stared back at his thin determined face. No more than a boy. Scarred by war. Captured. I should show some compassion.

'Are you ashamed of being German?' I said with a smile. 'You can hardly blame Rilke for Hitler.'

'I am ashamed of being myself,' he said.

He sunk down into the pew in front of me. He didn't look contrite. He put his feet up and rubbed his chin on the collar of his tunic.

'And you want to be someone else? Is that possible?'

An odd exchange in a cavernous conventicle never built to hear either English or German. Would it make for clarity? Remove everything to reach the bare bones of the truth.

'It is if I say so.'

He was resolved to rebuild himself from the floor up. He could change his name and he could change his language. He was young enough to start again. Perhaps he could manage it. For me it was much too late. I was buried alive in the past. He lay down on the pew bench as a place of clean comfort where it was possible he might snatch some sleep. I bent forward to look at him. With his eyes closed he looked more child-like than ever. The Colonel said he was a genius. That was a word I never understood the meaning of. Was this my chance to find out? His complexion was so soft he had hardly begun to shave. He had been through fire, and, I imagined, flattened to some form of insensibility. More than bringing him comfort, I wanted him to notice me.

'We all have our private pain to carry,' I said.

He showed so little interest he did not even open his eyes. I couldn't bear to sit there in silence until the Colonel saw fit to come back.

'Play some more,' I said. 'You play so well.'

He shook his head. It was too much trouble to open his mouth.

'In any case the Colonel said you should practice. So practice!'

He did not move. Out of the intense silence he began to talk to himself in German. I was there to overhear, as cool as an old priest in the confessional. We were surrounded by polished wood with a similar smell.

'He was better than me at everything. Music. Woodcraft. Cross-country. Weapon training. We joined the Hitler Youth on the same day. Reisiger, Horst. Rist, Klaus Wilhelm. Best of friends. Comrades and so on. He carried the phosphorous bombs. It was my turn to carry them. I was shivering with fear and I called it the flu. He carried them. Night attack. He was hit by something. Ten yards away from me in the corn field. It was cold. He was burning like a human torch. He screamed at us to shoot him. What else could we do?'

My hand was hanging over the side of the pew. He took it in both his and squeezed it so tightly I wanted to scream with the pain.

ii

He was in a state of high excitement. His hand was trembling as he held out the three air-letters all stamped *Censored* and *O.A.S.* The way his hand shook when he was nervous always made me uneasy. It seemed a flaw somehow. He was tall, fair-haired and healthy and he should have been above such lack of control. Four years of farm labour had given him muscle, filled him out, hardened his hands, but they hadn't stabilized his temperament. That was my view. Olwen was more tolerant. She accepted him as Meg's chosen friend. She said we should cherish him for his intelligence, and I suppose, the conscience that the Tribunal was allowing him to nurse on the land. It was alright for him to love and respect our daughter; to sit chatting to Olwen in the kitchen and play chess with me in the study. It was also much too soon to start treating Griff Kenyon as a future son-in-law.

'They want me,' he was saying. 'There's a place for me. These are from Dewi and this one is from Adam Rowntree. They are the team leaders. You can see they want me right away. I don't know what to do.'

We were standing in the empty cowshed at Hendrefor, a building of considerable antiquarian interest. We were surrounded by the smell of milk and cow-dung. All I could think of was, what an awkward time it was to be young. Not that he was all that young. At less than his age, young men have been dying all over Europe. And of course over the last four years no one could have been more acutely aware of that grim fact than Griffith Kenyon. It probably accounted for the trembling. He stood in his ragged working clothes as dedicated as a monk to poverty and hard labour.

'They are setting up a new camp for refugees in the old army barracks in Via della Scala. Seven or eight thousand displaced persons. There'll be another centre in Pisa. They want me there. They need chaps like me. Fit. Educated. Adaptable. Knowledge of machines and so on and the business of nutrition. Ready to work all day for nothing more than some kind of uniform and your keep.'

'Have you told them?' I said. 'In the house.'

'I don't know what to tell them. That's the trouble. They've been good to me. How can I leave them? You can see what he's like. Farmer's lung he calls it. Struggling to get his breath. This place is too big for them. The load would all fall on her. And old Ted couldn't cope with the Prisoners-of-war. They'd run rings round him. Bob Sling can't be relied on. What am I to do?'

It gave him some relief to shift part of the weight of his dilemma on to me. What else is a parson good for? The lad calls himself a fellow-travelling Quaker. He rides his bike once a Sunday to a market town twelve miles away where he attends some kind of service in a nonconformist chapel. We are broad-minded Olwen says, and we don't hold that against him.

'You must do what you think is right,' I said.

His large eyes stared at me as if I were heaping coals of fire on his head.

'Think of what you most want,' he said. 'And give it to someone else.'

It sounded like a quotation. He was young and it was quite possible his spiritual life was more intense than mine.

'The trouble is I've no one to give it to.'

That could only mean he was longing to go. Escape from one form of servitude to another. He was trembling because his mind was in a ferment. I understood from Olwen that Griff and Meg were incorrigible idealists. Last winter they were filled with the notion of creating a chain of kibbutzim from one end of Wales to the other. They were convinced that this would be the only way to keep a unique way of life alive. I kept quiet. They were looking at their country through rose-tinted spectacles. All the same I was moved by the purity of their devotion. Ideals make their greatest impact when you are young and eager and un-tainted by cynicism and disappointment.

'Do you want me to say anything?' I said. 'Shall I say something when I go in?'

This was a routine visit. Nell Parry was very faithful in church. Matins and Evensong. I watched her goitre oscillate in her neck as she spelt out the words of the hymns. Her voice was too thin to hear. She wore the same black hat, year after year. Emlyn stayed home. On the grounds of ill-health. He told Olwen once, in the most apologetic way, that being in church gave him a headache. She didn't know whether to laugh or sympathise, so she tapped him on the shoulder instead. It was true he wasn't strong. At the slightest indisposition he took to his bed. It seems his appetite was never affected. And Nell positively enjoyed loading a tray and carrying his breakfast to him in bed.

'Is he up yet?' I said.

It was easier to influence or persuade Emlyn Parry when he was in bed. Sitting in front of the kitchen fire, he was inclined to be stubborn and morose. Griff was shaking his head. He didn't want me to say anything.

'First I want to talk to Meg about it,' he said.

The child wasn't eighteen yet, for goodness sake. And he was holding forth like a dutiful husband about to consult his wife: and gazing at me in expectation of being commended for forethought and restraint. There were elements in their relationship that made me very uneasy. Her ambition had always been to go into general practice with her brother. A laudable and practical ambition. Hence the maths, phys, and chem, which she admitted she didn't really care for. She was prepared to struggle and I approved of that. Then along comes this breathless talk about oases and kibbutzim and the new monasticism to keep me awake at night. Olwen said it was just theory and talk. They argued that Western civilization was collapsing from within and that their mission in this world was to establish islands of self-sufficiency from one end of Wales to the other. 'Like the old Celtic saints,' Meg would cry out and wax lyrical about acorns and oak trees. Dangerous talk. I tried to pour scorn on it and they accepted my sarcasms as parsonical jokes. Maths, phys and chem for hermits, ... that sort of thing. When I had the chance I tried to demonstrate as clearly as I could that their notions were an unhealthy mix of parochial nationalism and utopian communism. Griff listened attentively and Meg said 'isms... isms...' in imitation of geese hissing. She was laughing in my face.

'Meg's very practical,' he said.

He gripped the hosepipe and the cane brush and waited for me to step aside so that he could begin cleaning out the cowshed.

Colonel Bacon crouched at the window of my little sitting room. The observation post he called it. He was so intent on his survey of the overgrown gardens and shrubberies all around the Residence that he was oblivious of the discomfort of his position. I had my albums out and the illustrated history of Schloss Lenz that was falling to pieces. One or two other items I thought would interest him. He was much more interested in our buildings. This place had once been the stables and the coach-house of a great country house. The mansion itself had long since crumbled away and it was his intention, he said, one day, to explore the woodland and mark out the lost foundations. 'A jolly good exercise' he called it. He radiated confidence and self-assurance even more than aftershave lotion. His arrival and his passage along the corridors had aroused curiosity and a satisfying ripple of excitement. I had raised my voice in order that he should raise his. I felt a half-forgotten urge to exercise some degree of authority. I had a whole range of amusing remarks in store. I restrained myself from making them. There was always a danger that they would deteriorate into complaint. He could see for himself that the rooms next to me were empty. They smelt of damp and were visited both day and night by mice and rats. There are few things more tiring to a man in his prime than the whine of a lonely old woman. Having him in my room at all was a triumph. He was sipping tea from the last undamaged cup and saucer of my Meissen. I had to move with particular care if I hoped to transform his passing interest into something approaching an alliance.

'Just look at the little devil. Genius or not, he's bone idle. Let's face it.'

The prisoner Klaus Wilhelm Rist was lying prone in the long grass. He could not easily be seen from ground level but from my window he was as exposed as an object just fallen from the sky. The other prisoners were more active figures in the overgrown landscape. There were two in the trees cutting overhanging branches and two more wielding sickles in the shrubbery. They would attack the grass on the lawns next, much of it grown to the height of unmown hay. K.W.R. was so motionless it occurred to me that he was pretending to be a corpse on the battlefield. He would lie like that all day until nightfall and the moonlight spread over him like a shroud. I thought of my ancestors and how many of them had been obliged to die on battlefields.

'What is it like?' I could not help asking. The Colonel was a military presence in my room.

'A battlefield,' I said. 'I was wondering what it was like.'

'I was in transport, Countess.' He smiled cheerfully. 'I never got nearer than the edges so to speak. God knows that was bad enough.'

I was so deeply in sympathy with the boy in the grass I felt I knew what he was thinking. Reliving the horrors. His friend in flames. The dead and the dying being swallowed by a red darkness. The terrible noise and the even more terrible silence.

'The poor boy,' I said. 'I think he is pretending to be dead.'

'Don't you worry about K.W.R., Countess. He's a clever little devil. He knows how to look after himself. Very entertaining and very glib. But you have to watch out for him. You should have heard him going on about the beauty of uncut grass. He said the Garden of Eden was uncultivated. Work was like Pride except that it came after and not before the Fall. Cheeky devil.'

The Colonel chuckled as he sipped his tea and knuckled his moustache.

'It's all over for him now anyway. We've still got the Far East to worry about. Our chaps are in Rangoon, but that's a hell of a long way from Tokyo, if you pardon the language. And then comes the real problem.'

He looked at me as if he was about to reveal a profound secret. Perhaps he was worrying about how to put the Humpty Dumpty Empire together again. Underneath the jolly surface it was the only thing an Englishman took seriously.

'Civvy Street. That's my problem. I don't fancy going back to a poky little office in the High Street. As I see it, there's a big future in Transport. After all they can't do without it, can they? It's not all over by any means, but a chap's got to think of his future. That's the way I look at it.'

He was giving me his smile and I suddenly became aware he wanted something. He wasn't here simply for the pleasure of my fascinating company. It was still my duty to entertain him. I pushed the book about Schloss Lenz closer to him and he began to look at it politely. My mother used to become so cross when she found me tongue-tied at parties and receptions. *You must learn to make the best of yourself Cecilia. Straighten up, won't you. And brighten up. Always be sure to have something interesting to say.*

'Do you care for duck shooting, Colonel?'

I don't know what made me say it. Maybe the blurred picture of the deer park and the vague memory of duck shoots. All those important heavy men, dressed up and well tended and potent and dangerous as their guns.

'Only with a bren gun,' Colonel Bacon said. I wasn't sure if he was joking. We were strangers after all, foreigners incapable of maintaining anything deeper than the most superficial lines of communication.

'I've been meaning to ask you, Countess.'

He looked up from the illustrations and put the question as though it had only just occurred to him.

'Did you know Lottie Litherland? Lottie Staisy as she was before she was married.'

He was expecting me to frown and recall. So I obliged.

'The Staisys. Something to do with coal and tankers. In Kiel and Hamburg. Jewish weren't they?'

'That's right of course.'

Colonel Bacon was delighted.

'She remembers you. I happened to mention I knew you. Litherland is something big in the Ministry of Fuel and Power. I don't know quite what, to be honest. But the rule of thumb is, if you've got connections you should use them. Perhaps we should get in touch?'

The man was much diminished in my eyes. And so of course was I myself. More of a fugitive than an exile. I could never see the Lottie Staisy's of this world again even if I wanted to. The Colonel was at it again.

'Do you know the Gethin-Wynnes?'

'I've heard of them,' I said. 'I don't know them.'

'Charming couple. Delightful place they have at Plas Idan. I know you like music, Countess. I wonder if you would care to attend one of their musical evenings. I would be happy to escort you.'

So much benevolence I had to accept at its face value like his smile. My instincts warned me to move with caution while my heart lifted up with the prospect of being considered socially useful again. I could be accepted and move in society even in my decrepitude.

'How very kind of you,' I said. 'After all there is nothing like live music.'

I pointed at my poor gramophone in the corner of my crowded little room.

iv

Nell Parry is an unsightly woman. Apart from her goitre her teeth have the disorderly aspect of a collapsed cromlech. I feel an immense sympathy towards her because I know she has a tender soul. And more than that. I share her peasant background to the extent that I can feel the permanent ache of hard labour in her bones. Her bent shadow was already on the rocks of my parish when homo sapiens first trod this corner of the earth. More than that her saintly patience reminds me of my mother and is therefore sacred. She sits on the edge of a kitchen chair with her elbow reaching towards the table and there are a dozen eggs cradled in hay in the basket balanced on her lap. She is waiting to offer them on the altar of our help.

'I try to make him comfortable,' she said. 'But he won't have it.'

'It's his conscience,' Meg said.

'Oh, I know that.'

Nell Parry knew all about Griff's conscience. We all did. At this very moment it was being inflated like an air balloon in the centre of our kitchen, obliging my daughter Meg to prowl around its perimeter and Olwen to press herself closer to the stove. For my part I was in the open doorway with the escape route to the study at my back.

'It's his choice to sleep in the stable loft,' Nell Parry said. 'Nothing but a bedstead, a table and a chair and a heap of books. He doesn't have to. Sweeps himself and throws wet tea leaves on the boards to keep down the dust. It's his choice. As far as I'm concerned he could have the best bedroom.'

Her eyes dart about more boldly than usual as she tries to decide whether to appeal to me as a recognised keeper of consciences or to Meg as the object of the young man's affections. She opts for Olwen as an impartial but benevolent judge.

'We don't want him to go. They can't all go and fight. There's got to be someone left to keep things going.'

'The fighting's finished,' Olwen said. 'The war's over. In Europe anyway.'

'That's what they say.'

I was amused and touched by the depth of her scepticism. Again she reminded me of my mother. At the end of the First War. *We don't know do we?* she used to say. *They only tell us what they want us to know and nine times out of ten it turns out to be false.* I knew what she meant by *they*. Inscrutable and unscrupulous worldly powers undermining divine providence, hell bent on one insane conspiracy after another to snatch the sceptre out of God's eternal hands.

'We need him,' Nell Parry said. 'Nobody needs him more than we do. He's in charge you may as well say. How could we manage without him? Emlyn treats him like a son. If you could speak to him, Rector. You could make him stay.'

The tears welling up in her eyes made me uncomfortable. I had no idea she had become so attached to the boy. It is always so difficult for a man to fathom the depths of the maternal instinct. Nell Parry never had children of her own. So the reservoir of mother love has been channelled to the fresh-faced youth banishing himself to the stable loft. His oversensitive conscience she would attribute to innate goodness. The condemnation of society in general would only deepen her inclination to protect him. He was the heir to her dreams and the last hope of Hendrefor. And now that very conscience she was prepared to cherish and defend was turning out to be no better than an enemy within the gates. A sleeping monster stirring in the manger. And so on. Analysis is a pleasurable process but it does nothing to assist one to arrive at a decision.

'We mustn't expect too much, Mrs Parry,' I said. 'I'll do what I can of course, but we must remember the young man has a strong will of his own. A will as well as a conscience. You may as well say one isn't much use without the other.'

I was tempted to deliver a brief homily until Olwen caught my eye. Without speaking she made me understand the woman was drowning in an emotional whirlpool and this was no time for rational discourse. There were large tear drops coursing Nell Parry's cheeks and I had to turn away from their unfamiliar beauty. I closed my eyes so that I was startled by the sudden sound of my daughter's voice.

'This is all nonsense,' she was saying. 'Of course he can't go. I'll go and speak to him this minute. It's his duty to stay here. Anybody can go off and join in clearing up the mess. Tinker, tailor, soldier, sailor.... Anybody. But he's the only one that can keep Hendrefor going. I'll go and speak to him. Where is he?'

Nell Parry was smiling through her tears. Quite lost in admiration for Meg's beauty and pugnacious attitude. It was a revelation. And then her face fell.

'He's locked himself in the stable loft. He says he doesn't want to speak to anybody.'

'We'll see about that,' Meg said. 'Don't you worry Mrs Parry.'

I felt there was something I should be saying. My daughter had grown up so quickly. I was half expecting her to ask my permission before riding off to Hendrefor on a Saturday afternoon. Olwen keeps telling me it was time I realised Meg was a young woman with a mind of her own. She kept telling me how much faith she had in our daughter's innate wisdom and discretion. All I could do was maintain an uneasy silence. In no time Meg was gone.

Nell pushed the basket of eggs along the table in Olwen's direction. I shuffled uneasily in the doorway. I was witnessing some kind of ritual that only took place between women when men weren't looking.

'They are so fond of each other,' Nell said. 'It's lovely to look at.'

I had retreated into the shadow of the corridor and was not meant to hear.

'They make such a lovely couple. As I said to Emlyn, at least they'll both have something nice to look at when they wake up in the morning.'

She clapped her hand over her mouth when she saw that I was still within earshot. I could hear them both laughing as I made my way down the corridor to the study.

THREE

i

He's not at all strong, you know,' Olwen said. 'Not really.'
I demonstrated restrained surprise. Griff Kenyon always appeared robustly healthy to me. Sulky. Preoccupied. For ever on his guard. Perhaps it was his mental health my dear Olwen was referring to?

'His father was badly wounded in the first war. Gas and shrapnel and goodness knows what. A difficult man. He died when Griff was eight I think. But you can imagine his suffering made an indelible impression on the poor boy's mind. And then his mother you see. Unbalanced really. Such a burden for a young boy to carry. She keeps a boarding house in Colwyn Bay. She had this complaint.... What do they call it? ....When you are afraid of going out of the house?'

'Agoraphobia,' I said.

'That's it! You are clever, Cecilia. Your mind is so clear. And you know so much. I'm really good for nothing except the kitchen sink.'

Looking at her making pastry in her kitchen confirms my belief that the truly beautiful are unaware of their beauty. She is middle-aged, but it is still easy to trace the uncommon loveliness of the daughter in the mother. That smile has the power of transferring the benevolent radiance of one being to another. They both have it. My own smile is a mere animal display of teeth of the same category as the snarl of a caged baboon or the shriek of a performing monkey. My mother used to urge me to smile more often. 'What's the point?' I used to say. I had read somewhere a stern look indicates sincerity. My mother accused me of being in a perpetual sulk.

'Meg can be so rigorous,' Olwen was saying. 'You have no idea. I can't think where she gets it from.'

I pointed discreetly at her breast and we both laughed. On the level of feeling there is no limit to the goodwill between us. How much we understand each other is another matter. She told me she always dreamt in Welsh. And I know I dream in German. So our communication is always in the second language. Yet it is detailed and sympathetic as it can only be between two women I would say wherever they come from. The morning sunlight turns the flour on her arms into gold dust and I have the urge to tell her everything or at least everything I would wish her to know. I love to watch the youthful energy in this woman defy the ageing process. She is pleased with her cold hands because they are good for making pastry. Hands are made for labour not for decoration. She can be cheerful and relaxed in the complete faith she shows in her daughter's innate wisdom and discretion. More than once I have heard her assert confidently that she did not think her Meg would do anything without telling her. Well, that could be true. This is an age that sets great store by frankness. It wouldn't have been much use to me in my youth: or much later for that matter. When I sit here and reminisce over a cup of tea it is an edited version of the past that I publish to amuse my dear Olwen who is willing to listen to me with such patience and unguarded pleasure.

'He listens too much to her,' Olwen said. 'And that gives her too much power. I'm not sure it's good for her.'

Yes. Well, the converse could be true. I was never impressed with this Griff of hers. I'd had to learn to curb my tongue after one or two efforts at oblique criticism. *Men are selfish creatures, Meg my dear. They can't help it. Even the best of them. It is in the nature of the beast. Listen to me, my dear. I speak from experience.* My humorous approach did not work. *I don't think anyone could accuse Griff of being selfish.* I made the mistake of an unconsidered reply. *Ah, I don't think anyone can accuse Master Kenyon of anything.* She was off without another word. It took several days if not weeks to regain my position in her affections. How could she know I was willing to sacrifice my cherished refuge in the Rectory kitchen in order to save her from her own generous girlish impulses? It went even deeper than that. I did not mind how much power the girl had over me, so long as she continued to exercise it. And that is as good a measure as any of the depth of an infatuation.

'This is ridiculous,' I said. 'But in some ways Meg reminds me of my grandmother.'

We were able to laugh again. I do so love the way Olwen laughs and listens. Her large eyes are so honest and trusting. Of course they have the same eyes. The mother and the daughter. Capable of so much interest in others. So much sympathy and understanding.

'Oma carried me off for the season. Meg's age but alas no beauty. An ugly duckling that never turned into a swan. They had no idea what to do with me. So off we went Oma and I. My Roman debut I suppose you could call it. But I wasn't the Belle of the Ball. Oma was. She had the money. My education or whatever was just an excuse.'

Olwen was so attentive I was ready to babble on all morning. Recapture the warm atmosphere of wartime: the blackout like a blessing obliterating the agonies of the outside world as we sat around the kitchen fire transforming the past into sequences of colourful bedtime stories.

'We stayed at the Hotel Elysee, opposite the Villa Borghese. I don't know whether you know it.'

She laughs aloud. Such honesty and charming innocence.

'Cecilia! I have never been out of these islands.'

'I mustn't bore you....'

'Goodness, no! I love to hear your stories.'

'Stories. That's all they are. The Past is a country we can no longer visit.'

I struggle to lace my memories with a little wisdom. However trite and second-hand it does not seem to diminish Olwen's willingness to listen.

'Rome must have been wonderful in those days,' she said.

'I was an excuse,' I said. 'Oma's real motive was a romantic love affair.'

'Your grandmother?'

Olwen was so charmingly surprised.

'When you think of it,' I said. 'She was older than I am now. Her title wasn't up to much but she had pots of money.'

'Pots of money.'

Olwen repeated the phrase as if it would have supplied her kitchen with rows of shining utensils of the latest design.

'A rich widow in love.'

'In love?'

'Yes, "in love" my dear. Old people are not exempt from the infection.'

We were laughing again and I was conscious of the privilege of being alone with Olwen and sharing her domestic warmth. To be in the Rectory kitchen was enough to change the quality of my life.

'But who was she in love with?'

'With a man almost as old as she was. Pushing sixty. Rather a useless old Sicilian *principe*. He used to send her flowers. Fresh flowers every morning. I can remember their sickly smell in the apartment. I used to think he was such a silly old fruit. So elaborate. Wax moustaches. He coloured his eyebrows. I would sit in the darkest corner of the room and imagine he was wax all over. Oma looked younger really. She was well preserved apart from her hair which had been fluffed once too often by her Viennese hairdresser and was getting distinctly thin on top. The *principe* had his box at the opera. I used to accompany them as a sort of underage chaperone. It was always Verdi or Puccini. I used to catch them making sheep's eyes at each other during the sentimental bits. There were all sorts of hints and whispers about the first time they met, goodness knows how many years ago, in some castle near Meran. He said "Merano" and she said "Meran". And this was supposed to have something to do with the cruel circumstance that had kept them apart for thirty or even forty years.'

'Oh dear. How sad,' Olwen said.

'Not a bit of it. Just a sentimental operatic fantasy. You never saw two people with their feet more firmly planted on the ground.

And then one fine day the grand opera came to an end.'

'What happened?'

'The *principe* asked if he could call at our hotel and introduce his fiancée.'

'Oh no.'

'She was a plump Sicilian girl under thirty. I remember he called her Giusi. We laughed about that afterwards. It sounded like juicy.'

'How did she take it? She could laugh later on obviously.'

'Awfully well. For one thing fat little Giusi was so respectful. As if she were being presented at court. Oma set great score by that sort of thing. She was a Victorian really. And the awful thing is in some way so am I. In 1945 for heaven's sake. Then Oma became suddenly tired of Rome. "These Italians," she said. "So superficial. Passing their entire lives posturing in the shadow of the relics of the mighty dead".'

'Goodness. Did she say all that?'

'Indeed she did. I was her captive audience. I was being maintained to listen, you could say. She would go on for hours. I learned a lot. That is why I am such a mine of useless information.'

'You should write your memoirs, Cecilia. You really should.'

This was always her way of applauding my frivolous anecdotes. My protective cover. All sins are relative. And the good rector assures us they are capable of being forgiven. My enemies have a more accurate assessment of my worth than my friends. I have been accepted and given shelter as some kind of anti-Nazi. The truth I can never tell. The class my family belong to flirted with that movement from the beginning and were more than ready to share in the benefits of its successes. People who live under false pretences turn cold at the prospect of being found out.

'Are you alright, Cecilia? You've gone very pale.'

I felt a smile twitch on my face.

'Somebody walking on my grave,' I said.

Meg came bustling in. Her face flushed, I assumed, from vigorous cycling. It was something I took to be her chief recreation.

She never looked more cheerful than when she was setting out on a journey of several miles, anywhere in this delectable region from the mountains to the sea.

'I was just telling Cecilia,' Olwen said. 'She really ought to write her memoirs.'

'Of course you should. It's your duty.'

Meg sat on a stool near the kitchen range. She thrust her legs out in a defiant pose. There was a brooding look on her face that her mother either did not notice or chose to ignore.

'Is there anything to eat?' Meg said. 'I'm famished.'

'Go and look in the pantry. You can see I'm busy.'

Meg emerged from the pantry carrying bread and margarine sprinkled with sugar. She leaned against the edge of the kitchen table more ready to talk having had something to eat.

'He's dying to go,' she said. 'And that is enough to hold him back. He rolls himself into a ball when he's distressed. Like a hedgehog.'

Pleased as I was to hear her speak of the saintly Griff in such a detached fashion, I had enough sense to restrain myself from further critical comment.

'What he needs is someone to talk to,' Meg said.

Her teeth sank into the bread as though she were determined to restore her energies as quickly as possible.

'He's got you to talk to,' Olwen said. 'Doesn't he talk to you?'

With practised speed she was cutting away the excess pastry off the apple pie on the plate.

'He just warbles on about his poetry, when I'm with him.'

I was delighted to watch her blush. My own heart was beating faster. I knew exactly how the would-be poet felt. No wonder he rolled himself into a ball. He found this girl swooningly beautiful, and nothing in his limited vocabulary could ever hope to do justice to her. He had to swallow his poetic pride. All the talk of his mastery of the strict metres and Eisteddfod prizes shrank into nothing confronted by the task of trying to celebrate one glance from those eager blue eyes.

'He's getting these air-letters from his friends. They arrive in one bunch and then they disturb him. He needs men of his own age to talk to. That's what he's missing. These letters just rub salt in the wound.'

'You should let him go,' Olwen said.

'Good heavens, you don't think I'm holding him back.'

It was always a privilege to sit at the kitchen table and witness their uninhibited friendly squabbles

'I think he should go,' Olwen said. 'It's a healthy life of course and in that sense it's done him the world of good. But times are changing....'

'It's a way of life, for heaven's sake. He chose it. He believes in it. Being at one with Nature is part and parcel of his philosophy.'

'The atmosphere there must be stifling. You've just said he's longing for someone to talk to.'

'He didn't say it. I said it.'

She was interrupted by the noise of a jeep driving into the stable yard. Meg peered through the kitchen window.

'Here comes the Occupying Power,' she said. 'The gallant Colonel and one of his slaves. He's getting very familiar. Dropping in at any time of the day or night.'

'Don't you start attacking him before he comes through the door....'

'Don't worry, mother dear. I've got better things to attend to.'

Meg marched out of the kitchen. I was wondering whether I should leave too.

As I struggled to my feet Olwen motioned that I should remain seated. The expression on her face suggested she did not wish to remain alone with the Colonel.

'Good morning, ladies. Good morning. I trust you will forgive the intrusion. Beware of the Greeks, what? Especially when they bring gifts. Shall we call it a small contribution to the church fête. To be used as you see fit.'

He deposited packets of sugar and dried fruit on the table. I took them to be army rations. He bent his knees and bowed to Olwen as if he were about to make an invitation to dance. She had to express the depth of her gratitude, but I could see from her eyes how amused she was by the Colonel's elegant manner, and the way he so obviously enjoyed the uniform he was wearing.

'Now then, dear lady. May I ask the most tremendous favour? As the Countess knows, that young creature squatting in the rear of my vehicle is by way of being something of a genius. Would it be too much to ask you to allow him to practise on your piano? The fact is I've jumped the gun a little. I offered him as a surprise item at the Gethin-Wynne's next Thursday evening, and the little blighter says he won't perform unless he can practise. That's one thing we haven't got in the camp and of course the chapel pipe-organ won't do at all. Dear Mrs Pritchard, do you think you could help?'

I heard the Rector's purposeful tread approaching down the corridor. Even before he arrived the Colonel had lifted his chin to present a propitiatory smile while Olwen swept the rations into the table drawer.

'Ah, Rector,' the Colonel said. 'Didn't realise you were at home. I was just telling your good lady I have the most enormous favour to ask. One of my inmates, should I call them? More talented than the rest. I wondered whether out of the kindness of your heart you would allow my musical genius to practise on your piano. A bit of an artful dodger, K.W.R., when it comes to hard labour but very conscientious as far as his artistic stuff is concerned.'

'K.W.R.?'

The Rector took his briar pipe out of his mouth to ask the question.

'Klaus Wilhelm Rist. He's got a number of course, but I can't remember it. He's very talented, isn't he, Countess?'

I could only nod. The Rector showed no interest in my opinion.

'We need to be positive,' he said. 'We need to get the best out of people.'

'That's splendidly kind of you.'

The Colonel assumed that permission was being given for the use of the piano.

'It hasn't been tuned for ages,' Olwen said. 'And the drawing-room is damp. We hardly ever use it.'

'At your convenience. I'll have him here under escort or I'll bring him myself. At such time as you see fit from now until next Thursday. He says he needs two hours a day. I'll tell him he'll take what he gets. And do his damnedest on the night or I'll have him in irons!'

He seemed to expect laughter all round. All he got was a wan smile from me. Olwen was intent on watching her husband as he sucked distractedly at his pipe. I had no way of telling whether or not the Colonel was aware of an atmosphere of unease. Perhaps his wartime rank permitted him to be professionally unaware of such niceties: like a tank that ploughs across the landscape without any concern for the havoc in its wake. For the first time I was seeing the Colonel as a threat rather than an amusing diversion.

ii

'What kind of music is that supposed to be?'

I found Meg standing outside the drawing room door. I was getting nowhere with my sermon and the din on the piano was no help at all. So much discordance and crashing chords and reverberations. At my desk in the study I'd had a stirring notion based on the disciples locking the door 'for fear of the Jews'. And I was preparing to make a sequence of striking inversions on the nature of persecution until the racket from the drawing-room sent my thought structures crashing to the floor.

'He has nightmares,' Meg said.

'How do you know?'

Even as I spoke I became aware how much my daughter had come to assume disapproval was my normal mode. This is what comes of having to be perpetually on my guard. My job is to warn my flock of the Lords of Misrule as well as the Terror by Night and the Arrow that Flyeth by Day. This is not the way at all I wish my daughter to see me.

'Griff told me. They talk. Klaus's English is very good. He gives Griff lessons in German and Italian, just in case.'

This sounded constructive enough. I needed to show some understanding.

'What kind of music is that?'

We listened together and it seemed to me the sound was crashing round the drawing-room like a wild animal trapped in a cage.

'His own composition, I think. Griff says he's a genius in search of his medium.'

Griff says this and Griff says that. How much people need to talk. Here I am within a yard of my only daughter with an immeasurable distance between us. If she needed to talk it would be to Griff she would turn, not to me. No doubt that is how it should be. This noise that gets on my nerves makes her look bright and alert. Also so naive and childlike that I am filled with a painful desire to protect her. My wife keeps telling me how exceptionally sensible Meg is, with a mind of her own, responsible, intelligent and so on. She would have me believe it as an article of faith. With such reassurances are our lives sustained.

Olwen was seated at the kitchen table, her sleeves rolled above her elbows and her hands red and wet. She was salting portions of half a pig I had been given by old Ben Davies Pen-y-Cefn. A loyal churchman if ever there was one. The salt water had splashed over an invitation card to a musical evening at Idan Hall. The Gethin-Wynnes if you please. Those would-be arbiters of taste and influence. She saw the expression on my face as I glanced at the card.

'Nice to be asked,' she said.

'You don't want to go?'

'Well it would be nice to hear the music.'

'You go if you want to....'

'I wouldn't dream of going without you.'

That was obviously what I wanted to hear. It enabled me to march about the kitchen in a confident manner and offer to make a cup of tea.

'I caught Meg lurking outside the drawing-room door listening to that awful row.'

Olwen decorated her automatic response with a mysterious smile.

'Meg is a very sensible girl. She has a mind of her own.'

'She should have her mind on her work.'

'She's bound to have her admirers. We must accept that. If she has a choice, let her enjoy it I say. Women never had a choice before. Not a real choice. The world is changing, Edwin. Changing fast now the war is over. It's time for a new beginning. Just imagine, maybe women will enjoy their share of freedom for the very first time.'

It puzzled me to understand what she was driving at. Was I supposed to look at her and see her trapped behind the kitchen table with her hands in bloodstained salty water? A still beautiful woman of forty-six, or was it forty-seven, voluntarily wearing herself out in the service of others.

'Edwin, be a good boy, and pull me some rhubarb sticks will you?'

I showed instant obedience. Gardening was something I could always be doing while my conscience gnawed at that which was left undone. The trouble with the duties of a parish priest is that they are never done: no beginning and no end, and always outlasting my limited supply of charity and loving concern. The wrong man for the job. The dew on the rhubarb leaves splashed all over my grey flannels. If there were such a thing as a woman priest, Olwen would do my job far better. For the simple reason that she was a better person. At least that was something I had learned from twenty-five years of marriage. I placed the sticks of rhubarb ready for use on the bare table and waited with canine patience for a word of commendation.

'It must be terribly difficult for men to understand.'

She was staring into the salt water in search of an answer to the riddle.

'And its difficult for women to find expression, in words that is, for things they understand perfectly well in their hearts. This world is packed full of things nobody mentions.'

'What things?'

Her mood was making me uneasy. She seemed to be peering over the edge into an abyss of relentless contemplation.

'Take sex, for example.'

She stared at me calmly.

'I know its something you are not keen on talking about.'

I tried to demonstrate extreme rational detachment without much success.

'The thing is you see, a man can ejaculate with almost any woman. Provided he isn't impotent, or homosexual perhaps? But a woman you see, once she has made her choice has got to stick to it. She has walked into a trap, you might say without trying to be melodramatic. A husband, children, a family. She can't move. She can't change. She daren't. But that doesn't stop her from experimenting in her imagination. If she's that way inclined. Of course she has to be subdued by the responsibilities of motherhood and so on but even they can't stop some women from being curious about what they may have missed.'

The serenity of her smile was more painful than a blow across the face. Surely there were things it were better not to look into too closely? Otherwise why should Eve have been punished for tasting the fruit of the forbidden tree? Why all this sudden appetite for choice? All this unbridled curiosity? It was something to do with the war ending and all this endless talk of a new beginning. New dispensations. Right and wrong must belong in the catalogue of absolutes like good and evil, definitions written on the tablets of the law. Otherwise I would be obliged to be constantly calling my vocation into question. And that would end in asking what right have we, my wife and I, to be living in this house. Or if it came to that, to exist at all? Olwen was a good woman and a good wife. How could I tell her that her brain power had its limitations and that she would be well advised not to venture into a minefield of dangerous speculations?

It was disturbing, irritating, to stand by the kitchen window and watch Colonel Bacon driving his jeep into our stable yard as if it were public property. He had acquired this ridiculous habit of approaching the Rectory via the back door. It really was up to Olwen to put a stop to it in one way or another. I was still formulating suitable phrases for her use as the Colonel called out in an absurdly coy voice and tapped one door after another as he made his entrance.

'Dear friends, Romans, countrymen, is our captive genius behaving himself? Is he practising hard?'

'I wish he would play more Bach. I love Bach,' Olwen said.

'Well then, Bach it shall be,' he said. 'Do you think Bach was a Welshman, Rector? Everyone seems to be "bach" around here.'

I wasn't going to laugh at his stupid joke. I wished Olwen wasn't so intent on being agreeable.

'Bach is so life-enhancing. That's what I love so much about him. He celebrates.'

Water splashed over the table as she made her enthusiastic gesture. I was determined to bring these sentimentalists down to earth.

'He was making the most awful row a few minutes ago. Not the kind of stuff that would go down at the Gethin-Wynnes' I should have thought.'

'Oh dear.'

The Colonel stopped looking so pleased with himself.

'I see I shall have to have a word with the lad. And I shall make it my business to lay on transport for you both.'

'I couldn't possibly go,' I said.

I had to try and sound as though I took no pleasure in being awkward.

'You may not know it, Colonel, but all this cultural activity is only a smoke-screen for political manoeuvres.'

'I don't follow,' the Colonel said.

'The Gethin-Wynnes are rabid Tories.'

'Ah. I see. We are Liberals here, are we? Sir Archibald and all that.'

He smiled as if to reassure us that his innate capacity for understanding would overcome most obstacles. I felt obliged to disabuse him.

'The debate in this household, Colonel Bacon, is between what you might call British Socialism and our Welsh national being. I know a clergyman is not supposed to parade his political affiliations, but between these four walls I can tell you we have no truck here with English Toryism.'

He was thrown but he looked more bewildered than upset. Perhaps I should have expressed myself more forcibly. I could see his jaw stretch with the effort of fabricating a tactful response.

'My dear chap, I am strictly non-political. My oath of allegiance is to the Crown of course. In times like these all I can say is we must do our best for the good of the country.'

I was about to ask which country when Meg came into the kitchen. The Colonel greeted her with cheerful formality, clicking his heels.

'Good morning, Miss Pritchard. I trust our musical prisoner is not causing too much of a breach of the peace.'

We could hear stormy noises in the distance. There were more comments I could make about the damage the young German was inflicting on our piano. If this was life-enhancing, what would life-destructing sound like? I was discouraged by the expression on Olwen's face.

'They ought to be sent home,' Meg said. 'Repatriated or whatever you call it. What's the point of hanging on now that it's all over?'

'You are absolutely right,' the Colonel said. 'I couldn't agree more. The sooner we get Jerry back on his feet the better. They've got a lot to offer. Not a popular view these days, I grant you. But it isn't all over, is it? I don't want to alarm you. You've still got your boy out there doing his bit. The Japs are still all over the Far East, and between you and me the Americans are an impetuous lot. All fire-power and froth. If there is such a thing as the white man's burden I'm afraid we're the ones that will have to carry it for quite a while yet.'

'I'm talking about human beings,' Meg said. 'Not Japs and Jerries.'

Olwen looked at me as if it were my duty to reprove our daughter for her over-assertive manner. For my own part I was prepared to listen. Give her a chance to develop a standpoint for which I felt an instinctive sympathy. After all, a minister of the gospel is supposed to proclaim we are all God's children, whatever our race or colour.

'He doesn't know whether his parents are alive or dead,' Meg said. 'That's the trouble. Hamburg was bombed to bits. He thinks the world of his sister. He thinks his mother must be dead. He hasn't heard a word from either of them for over a year.'

'How do you know all this?' Olwen said.

'Griff told me. They talk a lot together.'

'I'm all in favour of early repatriation, believe me,' the Colonel said. 'All the same you want to watch out for K.W.R. — take whatever he says with a pinch of salt.'

'What does that mean?' Meg said.

'They're not the same as us, are they? Foreigners and all that. You have to watch out for them. This one's as bright as a button and cunning to go with it. That's all I'm saying. It was always a funny old world, and now my dears, believe me, it's funnier than ever.'

iii

After the rain the sun burst through the clouds and the golden light flooded through the stained glass window. It wasn't an illusion. I sensed their mutual attraction before they became aware of it themselves. And it filled me with exultation. I saw two young people looking up at Adam and Eve being turned out of the Garden and the white beard of God in judgement above them. The light made them as beautiful as angels, my Meg and the suffering German boy. She was looking at him with such tender concern and I could share it. He had been through so much and yet he was still a boy. There was a tension in his body that called out to be soothed. The wisp of a brown moustache only drew attention to his youth. His high cheekbones needed to be touched. The mute yearning in those wide eyes needed to be assuaged. It would happen, and I would watch from a distance a magical process that had never happened to me. I would feel no envy. Only a sense of overwhelming joy. I could have embraced them both and led them to the narrow altar in search of a blessing. Instead I stood guard by the unlocked open door.

This chapel of ease was in the grounds of a ruined mansion which had served as a soldier's sanatorium, I was told, during the first war, before falling into disuse. The chapel had been built over a hundred years ago by a guilty landowner after six men had been crushed to death in one of his quarries. I have become enamoured of this countryside and this country. Because of this girl, I suppose, I am able to feel a genuine affinity with it all. In high summer the desolation of the great house takes on a splendour of its own. And outside beyond the village I am willing to lose my way in the abundance of by-ways that wind through banks and hedgerows heavy with their own wild harvest. Every undulation hides more hamlets, charming hollows and warm retreats. A land for love. Behind us the high drama of the mountains and before us the restless colours of the sea.

In a corner of a wood bordering the park the Rector and the conscientious objector, armed with sickles and billhooks, are clearing a corner in search of a lost memorial stone. The Rector is convinced from old church records that it lies somewhere there. He knows it is inscribed with rude Roman capitals and a cross inside a circle. He is determined to recover it. I never saw the man look so resolute. I can well imagine this whole country is full of hidden treasure. He looks at me less sternly when I pay close attention to his exposition of the complexities of local history. I can hardly tell him that it is the sight of his daughter with this German lad that has given it all a new centrality and meaning for me. To look at them provides a new solace to the dull ache of my isolation that has been augmented rather than diminished by the ending of wartime restrictions. I must content myself with second-hand spectator pleasure and at all times exercise a restraint that is so alien to my own impetuous nature: the length of a lifetime and such a catalogue of mistakes to learn such a simple lesson: try not to interfere.

The empty church is their elected space. They are standing dangerously close together. Perhaps I should make them more aware of my presence. I am old and they are young and they should know of their awesome capacity for creating an hermetic world of their own. It is in any case a civilising process to bring young and old closer together. That is sufficient excuse. Let it atone for my illicit urge to participate more closely in whatever was happening to them. Klaus was staring hard at the stained-glass window.

'Hideous,' he was saying. 'Absolutely hideous. A complete disaster. Just like everything to do with religion.'

'Why do you say that?'

I could see that if Meg was going to help him she would have to understand the condition from which he suffered. All the same I was disappointed. Perhaps there was no more than a division of labour involved after all. Griff Kenyon was helping her father and she was attending to his friend. The friendship between the conscientious objector and the Prisoner-of-War was something generally approved of at the Rectory. I had to recognise how much I nursed a secret hope that the attractions of Klaus Wilhelm Rist would wean the girl away from her premature attachment to the moody self-absorbed Griff Kenyon. It was not my place to stage-manage these youthful friendships. My previous experience was irrelevant and yet I was harassed with a desire to help.

'Religion is man-made. So it has to be a disaster. Like that stupid white beard. Men make gods in their own stupid image. They spread them around. Spreading religions is like peddling a plague.'

'There's no God. That's what you are saying.'

'Almighty Death. That's all we need to worry about.'

- 51 -

'So you think my father is wasting his time?'

He grins at her with that lopsided charm I find so appealing.

'If it keeps him out of mischief....'

What could I do but turn away? My sentimental vision evaporated. Like so many of my reveries and dreams this one was as false as a mirage. I would be better engaged watching the Rector's efforts with his sickle and the muscle power from his farm-labourer conchie. At least they were digging for some form of reality. And there would be genuine triumph when they recovered it. Memorial stones meant something. Tokens of respect however old. I should nurture a greater curiosity about the vanished race that put them up. But first I had to keep my thoughts to myself and watch the Rector's triumph and share his satisfaction in silence. He had found it. The inscription was face downwards. I stood back to admire the tender care he took to uncover the inscription and trace out the letters with his earth-caked fingers.

They needed Klaus's help to move it. He came running and Meg followed him with her arms folded. It was too heavy to move. The Rector shook his head before he decided to leave it where it was for the time being. Once more he knelt down to trace the incisions on the stone.

'Late fifth, early sixth century.'

He delivered his verdict with such reverence it made Klaus Rist smile. The Rector caught him smiling. He resented his diagnosis being taken so lightly.

'There were Christians here when your Teutonic tribes were still wandering barbarians. Destroying and slaughtering everything on sight.'

By the end of the afternoon I was thoroughly depressed. It had been an excursion I had so looked forward to. I was foolishly dreaming of a romantic relationship blossoming between my Meg and the Prisoner-of-War. When that happened everything would take a turn for the better. Somehow a new understanding would have emerged in the wake of the dream between the Rector and myself. Instead of that, I felt his hostility to anything

German intensify. I became afraid of opening my mouth. And fear is a degrading condition. Even Meg for whom I feel such unconditional affection seems preoccupied: distant and indifferent. When the Rector put me down at the gates of the Institution for Decayed Gentlewomen I was filled with a sense of abandonment and isolation.

It is possible that the fault lies in my nature. I was disadvantaged at birth and by birth. My parents had no affection for each other. My governesses bullied me. They favoured my sister who died so beautifully from consumption at the age of nineteen. My only talent has been for survival and this is where it leaves me. A crippled animal hobbling back to her lair. The voices of the persecutors are all around me. And their stones. A pebble struck the back of my neck with cruel force. I swung round to see the caretaker's children turn tail and disappear into the bushes. The smallest was the slowest. Wayne, they called him. Five or six years old. He had a more malevolent sister, Sandra, aged eight who told one of the stupider inmates that she was going to be a witch when she grew up. She threw it. Egged on by her sneaky older brother Denzil, who crept around the residence sniffing around old women's knick-knacks for anything he could pinch with impunity. Was I to stand for it? By no means. I made my way to the caretaker's lodge.

I pounded the door with the handle of my walking stick. No one answered. She knew perfectly well I was there. I pounded again. The door opened suddenly and I was confronted by the woman's bony face. Her sleeves as usual were rolled up to draw attention to the fact that she was in the midst of her never-ending labours. A smell of stale stew blasted into my face. It was summer but her lazy good-for-nothing father-in-law was crouched over a blazing fire sucking at his disgusting pipe. The fire was there so that he could spit into it. Always the biggest fire in the whole place, burning away while old women shivered away in their cheerless rooms.

'Those children of yours, Mrs Melling!'

I struggled to keep the screech out of my voice.

'They are at me throwing stones.'

My command of English idiom is always at its shakiest when addressing this insolent woman.

'Dear me,' she said.

She was enjoying the spectacle of my anger. I had to make a greater effort to control myself.

'Am I to stand of it?' I said. 'By no means.'

She makes no attempt to apologise.

'And that eldest boy you have....'

'He's got a name,' she said.

'Only three days ago I caught him red-handed going through my things.'

'I can't be everywhere,' she said. 'And I can't do everything. Their father is away fighting for his country, which is more than you can say for some of the folk round here. I'll say no more than that.'

'I will have my key and I will keep my key. There will be no one in my room unless I am there.'

'Please yourself,' she said. 'I expect things will be changing around here very soon.'

I watched her lift my key off the row of hooks. Her father-in-law seemed amused by what was going on. He spat in the fire and cleared his throat. The dregs of some kind of a meal was still on the table. The woman was a self-righteous slut. I could not endure the way she handed me the key.

'You had better keep an eye on those children,' I said. 'If you don't they'll be inside a gaol before they reach twenty years old.'

She slammed the door in my face. I could have thanked the woman for her hostility. Strangely it lifted my spirits. I still had the strength to resist, the capacity to sharpen my defensive weapons. The rain was falling again. I would not allow it to dampen my spirit. I could still prepare myself a frugal but nourishing meal and wind my ancient gramophone. I would not allow my moods to correspond too closely to the vagaries of the Welsh weather. I had sallied forth in a sunburst of triumph: now through my narrow window the dripping leaves were dangerously close to girlish tears and distant disappointments.

Music was always my friend. What I needed was a little redeeming love and it came on demand through the sound-box: a soprano sharing her tender declaration with me: *Du bist die Ruh*.... You are tranquillity and gentle peace, you are desire and satisfaction.... 'Ah Cecilia,' Olwen would say. 'You had so much. You have so many memories.' And she accepted my reply — 'I have known great wealth and great poverty' — as a revelation of an untold depth of experience, while I knew it covered a lifetime of nothing worth summing up. My past was nothing wonderful. I had never known great days yet there must have been moments. I listened to the music with desperate intensity in the hope of reliving some simple thing, some illuminating fragment from those distant days.

The cathedral echoed with those powerful voices. Afterwards we ran across the frozen lake, all of us in love with the moonlight and the mesmerising glitter of the stars. We were young and everything was possible, and the music still reverberated in our heads like an order of release. One of the girls said to me, '"When you listened did the skin tingle on the back of your neck?" She spoke with childish honesty. I loved her and now I cannot even remember her name. Fountains of moonlight rolling.... Such silly words, such thrilling sound.

Someone was knocking at my door. Ready to intrude. Eager to wreck my privacy.

'Turn that thing down.'

I struggled to turn up the volume on my machine and make Bruch's *Jubilate* swell up even louder.

'Stop that awful row, will you!'

Letitia Hughes-White. Who else.

'There are other people living here. Have some consideration.'

She paused and knocked the door again. I was so pleased it was locked. I have no weapon to confront the murderous hostility. Silence was my only defence.

'Don't think you will get away with this. It will be reported to the Committee. You won't get away with it. You won't. You won't. You German fraud.'

FOUR

i

'We've got two weeks to save the world,' she said. 'That's what it amounts to.'

I don't know where the girl gets this fury of enthusiasm from. Her mother I suspect. Several wild idealists in that family. Bright but unrestrained. Now her exams are over she emerges from three weeks of intense work and a silence that was positively sulky, ready to challenge the fabric of the established order. Griff and the candidate were staring at her with open admiration. Her eyes were wide and shining. They could see she was beautiful of course, and disturbing. She had invaded my study specifically to disturb. She had brought it about. One of those unnerving occasions that oblige me to vouchsafe a yea or a nay without the appropriate time to make a considered judgement. My daughter refused to acknowledge that I was a man who had taken holy orders in order to be allowed to meditate and not to be forced to make instant irrational choices. The candidate himself was another enthusiast but older and more circumspect in his manner.

'If you could see your way, Mr Pritchard,' he said. 'Mind you I know just how you feel....'

It was possible he did. He was, I suppose, a reputable scholar: certainly a prolific author of what I tended to regard as somewhat unconsidered works. A tall, thin restless fellow who needed a lot of elbow room. He had this torrential no-time-to-waste South Wales way of talking that would be more of a hindrance than a help in this constituency. A man driven by a mission and given to manifestoes is fated to suffer a hard time among our taciturn not to say truculent natives.

'I felt exactly the same when they approached me to accept the nomination. "Why should I," I said, "just because my name is Llywelyn?"'

I was supposed to smile at this unsubtle joke. Meg and Griff were standing behind him quietly insistent that I should give him the same rapt attention.

'Find a younger man with fewer responsibilities,' I said. 'This is a general election at the worst possible time for me with mountains of marking to attend to. And what about my family? And what about transport? I don't even possess a car.' I gave way at the third time of asking. They wore me down with their third time for a Welshman. 'But my dear sir, your daughter is absolutely right. This is a time to rebuild our little world. The time of the breaking of the nations is over. There has been a fundamental realignment of power in the world. I had to ask myself the simple question as we all have to at this moment in time. Who will stand up and speak for Wales? For Wales and not for the great English party machines. How will we ever count if we do not speak up for ourselves?'

It was an argument with which I was in broad agreement, only I wished Meg and Griff would stop nodding like a pair of ventriloquist dolls. They were so uncritical lapping up a message they were longing to hear.

'The Liberals? They are dead from the neck up. Labour? A party machine intent on massaging the masses with promises in order to capture and monopolise the levers of power. The Conservatives? English imperialists to a man. Dedicated to preserving their Empire in some kind of historical formaldehyde.'

These were plainly observations and pronouncements he was hawking around the country from public meeting to public meeting. Did I detect a youthful ambition to be a popular preacher re-emerging? He was hoarse with repetition of his own brand of urgency. The man was sincere. He was honest and seeking no possible personal advantage except perhaps the consolation of occasional perfunctory applause. He was laughing now at the unstoppability of his own eloquence. Meg and Griff were looking at him with reverent affection. It struck me how quickly the young respond to unpretentious humility. And how irrelevant such a quality is to the career of the politician.

'I get carried away,' he said. 'But it keeps me going. As I see it Mr Pritchard, we have to carry our message to as many people as possible in as short a time as possible. This isn't easy. Not just for lack of transport. It isn't easy because our philosophical base is so different from the others.'

'Yes,' I said, as judiciously as I could. 'I was about to ask you about that.'

'Well now. I hold that Politics should be among the highest arts.'

'Do you really?'

I tried not to sound sceptical.

'Yes, I do. We need to combine the ideal of a Republic and the fundamental Brotherhood of Man with the unique value our Christian gospel attaches to the individual soul.'

He was leaning towards me with a look of triumph on his face. I was a man of the cloth and his argument was compelling me to agree with him in a way that I could easily have resented.

'The first aim of political action is to bring the strength of the gospel into the domain of public affairs. And that is why we approach you in the first instance. Will you chair our public meeting in the village hall tomorrow night?'

I had to answer. Outside a weary student was sitting at the wheel of a battered Austin Twelve, ready to carry our hero by fits and starts to his next meeting. It was a hopeless cause. Chasing all over this scattered constituency from one schoolroom or hedge-top to another. Attractive to students maybe, and the enthusiastic young like Griff and Meg, but anathema to people of importance. Why should I be involved at all? The silence in the room was not a silence to savour. I was uncomfortably aware of a host of difficulties I could not name aloud without gaining the contempt of my daughter. I could not even ask for more time to consider the request without sounding like a man desperately in search of excuses. What could I say except 'yes'.

There was no time for reservations. I wanted to add that I would take the chair in order to ensure that he had a fair hearing: was given an opportunity to put his case; but that did not mean

I had decided to speak in public on his behalf or even to vote for him. He held my hand in both his and shook it vigorously. I was aware of the chill in his bony fingers. He was not a strong man in spite of his height. His cheeks were feverish and his eyes were red, it seemed to me, from lack of sleep.

'Heartfelt thanks,' he said. 'And now I must away in our chariot of fire. We are dreadfully late as it is.'

He departed, still paying out biblical phrases about the extent of the harvest and the shortage of labourers. Whether it was a clarion call or not it set my heart beating at a faster rate. It had me rushing through my books all that afternoon in search of texts: indulging a lifetime's weakness for seizing on quotations and trying to squeeze them into emerging situations. *Then Kei stood up and said whoever wishes to follow Arthur let him be with him in Cornwall this night. And those who do not...* which only gives rise to a subsidiary problem. This gangling awkward hoarse-voiced fellow is not Arthur by any stretch of imagination even if his name is Llywelyn. Every quotation I unearth is inapplicable. So what are all these books good for if History insists on never repeating itself? Why drag in Athens and Sparta or Carthage and Rome in order to render the chaos of the present intelligible? A present moment is chaotic by definition. It is only when events are over and done with that they make themselves available for interpretation and by then it is all too late.

In any case I am under no obligation to sing this fellow Llywelyn's praises or make exaggerated claims for the man or his mission. The contemplation of the historic past shrivels me up with my own insignificance even in this limited parochial context. Such virtue as may belong to modesty or self effacement also disappears. All I can do is keep a cool head, demonstrate a trace of educated intelligence by a show of impartiality indistinguishable from indifference: present, preside, conduct the proceedings and call the house to order if the occasion arose. That was all there was to it, so why should I suffer twenty-four hours of nervousness culminating in a bout of indigestion on which a final dose of Bisodol made no impression.

'Are you coming?'

I spoke to my wife with studied calm. Olwen sat by the window of our bedroom, sewing by the evening light, with her spectacles on the end of her nose. Make do and mend. My wife was never idle.

'You do whatever Meg tells you to do, Edwin, and you won't go far wrong. That girl never ceases to astonish me.'

'Why?'

'Besides, she has a longer lease on the future than we have.'

Against the light Olwen's dark figure could have been one of the Fates, sewing instead of spinning. Even as I watched she used her teeth to break a thread. My wife and my daughter have access to a depth of understanding well out of my reach. Often when they smile or laugh at me I am unnerved and such self-confidence as I possess evaporates.

'It wouldn't be so amazing if he won,' she said. 'Even though it is totally unlikely. That doesn't make sense, does it? But you know what I mean. After all ninety-four percent of the constituency is Welsh-speaking. Of course politically that doesn't mean anything either. But that's not the point. There are few things more admirable in this world than a Lost Cause. It's so dignified somehow. Romantic even. Am I talking nonsense?'

'Are you coming? I shall need to bring out the car. It looks like rain.'

And use my precious petrol ration. An uncovenanted contribution to Mr Llewelyn's parliamentary aspirations.

'I tell you what you could do,' Olwen said. 'You could drop me off at the Institution. Cecilia hasn't been at all well, the poor old thing. Not that she's that old. I just get the impression sometimes the poor thing is worn out. At the end of her tether.'

If your own wife and daughter are a mystery to you, how can you hope to understand anyone else? If we have no means of 'knowing' there are no real foundations to our existence, and therefore we have no control over our circumstance. Everything that appears blindingly obvious is at the same time impenetrably obscure. This is what becomes of being a country parson with too much time for thinking. The world is a kaleidoscope of colourful but unrelated facts. The slightest shake and your individual existence is obliterated and a new pattern asserts its inscrutable self-existence.

Olwen opens her umbrella and the scruffy Lodge children scatter in front of her like startled chickens. I can see their mother peeping behind their grubby lace curtains ready with her latest grievance. From Olwen she retreats. She prefers to address her complaints to me. My engine was ticking over and I was glad to press on. I had a role to play. I was a little late, in fact meetings like this never start on time and I had my parochial duties to enumerate if any excuse is needed.

Rain retarded my journey. Outside the village hall it was bucketing down. On the verandah four or five men in their shirt sleeves were leaning on a piano they had been pushing and pulling, staring gloomily at the sheets of rain. Inside some kind of a meeting was in progress: a public monotone in what had to be a meagerly attended meeting.

'Rotten night, Rector. This is on its way to the British School. Welcome home for the local lads, back from the army. Pity about the weather, but what can we do? You won't be seeing many in here. Better off with us, Rector....'

It is part of the nature of my office as I see it, never to look flustered or taken by surprise. These men were all nonconformists but we had the weather in common.

'What about the election, men? What about the future of the country?'

I felt obliged to put the question and I did so with a friendly and forgiving smile. I had a reputation for broad-mindedness and tolerance to maintain.

'Don't suppose it will make much difference to us, Rector bach.'

Neither hot nor cold. A stoic indifference. It was something I could understand. Part of the temperament of this part of the world. There was a line I could insert almost anywhere in the more recent passages of my unwritten parish history. *This green land of such beauty blest with diffidence and inertia....* At what point in the ever rolling stream of time did these characteristics enter their bloodstream? Should I blame the Tudors? That was becoming the fashionable thing to do.

When I appeared at the back of the hall the speaker raised his voice and warmed to his task. He was a small plump Baptist minister with tousled fair hair and spectacles that looked as if they had been painted on his face, they fitted so closely. His audience consisted of three schoolgirls in the front consuming their sweet rations; two elderly farmers who appeared to be enjoying the oratory, Albert the butcher and his backward son and a line of five middle-aged women who kept nudging and looking at each other as if they were not certain they had come to the right place. Democracy at work.

'My dear friends, I am here to hold the fort until the next speaker arrives and then I move on as fast as I can to my next port of call. That's the way we do it and what else can we do? Poor but proud and pure in heart. And I want to leave you with the very essence of my message. Something for you to remember in your hearts. Vote, my dear friends, for the little party that is your party and nobody else's. The party of the princes and the poets and the preachers. There you have three 'p's' easy to remember. The princes for freedom and independence — the poets for celebration of a better life, — the preachers to bring us visions and give us moral fibre.... Ah, Mr Pritchard, Rector of this ancient parish, thank you for coming. Shall I carry on?'

I responded to his anxious waving as though they were cries for help. On the platform we shared a muttered consultation watched by our scattered audience, animated with a fresh spurt of curiosity.

'My dear friend, thank you so much for coming. Thank you for showing what side you are on in these difficult times.'

He breathed warm sincerity into my face. Minister of a minority Baptist chapel in another corner of the county, said to live on a starvation stipend and still able to run an Austin Seven.

'Shall I carry on, or is it time for questions? So much ground to cover. In so little time. It's thin here tonight, I'm sorry to say. And the weather's against us. But what can we do?'

I asked for questions. For an interminable minute there was no response. At last one of the farmers stirred in his seat. Only then did I notice his sheepdog lying between his feet.

'I am an old Cymro who wants what is best for his country. I'm not afraid to say as much as that.'

His voice had a deep rich tone and I could see he and his dog liked listening to it.

'I hear what you are saying, brothers. Princes, poets, preachers. I'll remember that. It's very good. But I have a question. A simple question. Tell me, brothers, who is going to pay for it?'

It was a fair question. I suppressed an unworthy longing to be elsewhere. I turned to the zealous Baptist inviting him to answer it. His mouth was already open and his fingers raised to outline what he called his party's 'five point economic plan', when an angular woman in a raincoat appeared in the open doorway waving a wet umbrella and demanding to be heard. It was my duty to call her to order. She was a female I could recognise but not immediately put a name to.

'Up to your dirty tricks again!'

Her voice was shrill with the effort of making her voice sound indignant.

'Make a note of this good people. These are Nationalists at work. It was the spirit of nationalism that built those camps in Germany. Make a note of it.'

When we take a decision to act even on such a constricted stage we have to accept the consequences however awkward. I would have to reason with this woman and I had no idea how to begin. I had to exercise a function as chairman of this desultory meeting. The Baptist minister could not contain himself.

'Now then Miss Carlin Thomas. Now then. Now then. Let us try to be fair, shall we? We are all Christians here, so let us have no wild slinging of mud.'

'Dirty tricks, what else?'

Now I remembered who she was. A part-time W.E.A. lecturer.

I set up a class for her in the next village, one winter during the war. She opened her raincoat and I caught a glimpse of a massive red rosette. In the name of educational impartiality I could calm her down and point out on how many issues we were on the same side.

'This hall was booked for Labour. The candidate and his party will be along any minute. It's my job to keep the meeting going till he arrives, so out you Nationalists go and take your nationalism with you! Out! Out!'

She waved a paper under my nose as her title deed to possession of the floor. The Baptist and I were exiled to the verandah. When his indignation had sufficiently subsided, my companion began to press me to accompany him to his next assignment.

'Think of the impression it would make, friend. We need more recruits from the established church.'

I did not feel obliged to tell him the Church in Wales had been disestablished a quarter of a century ago, or to accompany him. Who said momentous events were no more than the accumulation of trivial occasions? Few occasions could have been more trivial than this one. In a moment the Labour candidate rolled up as if to confirm this impression. His vehicle was surprisingly large. He was flanked by aids and agents who were there to cosset him and ease his progress. One of the followers jumped down to peep into the hall and returned to report on the size of the meeting. The car engine was running and I could hear their voices raised. They were all cheerful and confident and passing humorous remarks about Miss Carlin Thomas. It was the candidate himself who decided to drive on to the next meeting without informing her. 'Comrades,' I heard him say. 'It's votes that count, not people. Let her offer up her voice on the altar of the Cause.' There was much sniggering and suppressed laughter as they drove off. The candidate smiled and waved at me as a possible vote. My Baptist colleague was quite annoyed with me for waving back.

At home in the empty Rectory I consoled myself with a cup of tea. To be so keenly disappointed I must have dreamt at some point during the last twenty-four hours of scoring an oratorical success: and exercising an inspired eloquence, arousing a sea of eager faces to respond to my clarion call. What faces and what call? My parishioners of course, and the call of love of country that would rise above denominational differences. All those nonconformists would welcome their shy and retiring Rector by acclamation. And be guided by him to the white vineyard at the gates of the Promised Land.

Someone was pulling at the front door bell. It sounded like a summons. I was coming to the conclusion that I had no stomach for electioneering. I had lived too long in a condition of unhealthy passivity. What possible good were the best of intentions if they were not alive with passionate intensity? I was paralysed by a sense of timid inadequacy. The bell rang again. I had to steel myself merely to answer the door. It was Bates, Sir George Ellis Owen's cockney chauffeur. The old Daimler was parked several yards down the drive.

'Sir George, would like a word,' Bates said. 'He says if you would be so kind. His leg's playing him up, he says.'

The accent grated on my ears. Since the end of the First War Bates considered himself 'Stationed' at Pentir Hall. He was employed chauffeur-handyman on the strength of his left arm slow bowling. Sir George had a passion for cricket. All so pleasant on a summer afternoon. And the leaves rustling overhead when one popped into the trees beyond the boundary for a pee. One of the pre-war pleasures to look back on with nostalgia during 'the dark days of the war', as the papers had already taken to calling them. Were they so bad? At least life was simpler. And we all learned to live on less.

'Look here, Pritchard, what's all this I hear about you?'

I held an umbrella in one hand as I offered him the other. He didn't take it.

'You don't expect me to shake hands with one of the conchie party's supporters, do you?'

I wanted to ask him if there would be any cricket before the end of the summer. Probably not, because of the war in the Far East. Bates was peering ostentatiously under the far side of the car bonnet and using his long ears to pick up our conversation. He was known at the Hall as a master of backstairs intrigue.

'Now it's all over they come creeping out of the woodwork,' Sir George said. 'And what did they do towards the war effort? Damn all except get in the way. What on earth do you think you're up to, Pritchard?'

'Exercising my right to free speech,' I said.

My heart was thumping but I smiled and tried to sound as reasonable as possible.

'It won't do you any good, you know. With the people that count. Here we are trying to put the things that matter back where they should be and you go out preaching red revolution, or whatever it is these impossible people want. The more upsetting the better, the way they look at it. No gratitude. That's the trouble with people nowadays. Old Winnie saves their bacon, your bacon too Pritchard, and now they can't wait to kick him out. And let me tell you something else for your own good, while I'm at it. You want to curb that daughter of yours. I know your boy is out there doing his bit, but that doesn't give her the right to go rushing around the place preaching her miserable Welsh conchie gospel. I'll say no more than that. A word to the wise, eh? And no hard feelings.'

This time it was he who held out his hand. I breathed deeply, shook my head and walked as steadily as I could back to the house.

ii

There was something about the woman that made me grit my teeth. She gushed effortlessly. When Colonel Bacon introduced me as the Countess Cecilia von Leiden she held on to my hand and trilled, 'But where have you been hiding?' 'In an old people's home,' I snapped and surprised myself by sounding so ungracious. Charm costs nothing. On the other hand I never had much to spare.

'The Honourable Angharad Wynne,' Colonel Bacon said.

He wasn't at all short of charm. He and our hostess sprayed each other with generous quantities of home-made allure.

'Call me Winkie,' she said. 'Everyone else does.'

This gave her the opening to tell me what happened in the third form at Roedean. A temporary tick in her left eyelid. She had been Winkie ever since, and she and the Colonel found the anecdote quietly hilarious. He even managed to suggest that the temporary affliction had contributed to the abiding beauty of her eyes. She trembled inside her thin frame at the compliment. Angharad Gethin-Wynne. In spite of their names and their ancestry this was a class of Sudeuten English marooned on their properties, fortified with nick-names and illustrated magazines. Were we any different? Oma had a cousin stuck out somewhere in the Ukraine she called *Putzi* and another one in Denmark, a big fat man she called *Hoernchen*. I forget their names and their titles and remember their nick-names. I hope they are safely dead. Like the aristocratic network they belong to. How long will this lot manage to carry on?

I was required to say hello to Mummy. She was quartered within earshot of the music room and her wheelchair was parked alongside her bed. She was propped up on pillows consuming a large helping of raspberries and cream. On the table beyond her bed was a bottle of gin and a phial of Angostura bitters. She waved her spoon at me.

'Pour me a drink,' she said. 'And make one for yourself. Where were you on September 3rd 1939?'

She was cunning and she smelt. For this musical occasion she had been heavily made up but not washed. Where had I been that day? As if I didn't know. In a chemist's shop in Norbury, wishing I were in the Outer Hebrides, wondering how far down in the world I had come. Buying aspirins and liquid paraffin for Tom's three impossible aunts. He had dumped me there while he went chasing after another unattainable film deal. Another spark flying upward. Who would ever listen to him and his glib exaggerations, his name-dropping recitals. He had only to open his mouth and exhale cigarette smoke through extended nostrils for you to know he was a liar. The voice of Mr Chamberlain from the room behind the chemist's counter was more in keeping with the dreary truth. *I have to tell you from such and such an hour … the world as we know it has come to an end.* Those endless tedious streets and that endless tedious voice belonged to each other in welded wedlock.

'Well. Where were you?'

'In London.'

I used the place name with some deliberation in order to command this smelly old woman's respect. Her hub of the universe.

'I can't get around any more,' she said. 'No petrol. And the trains are so dirty.'

I don't know by what right I looked down on this self-elected élite. I was the shabbiest of the shabby among them. Threadworn like an old carpet. I might have made more of an effort if Olwen had agreed to accompany me. She resisted the gallant Colonel's blandishments and at the same time urged me to go. 'It will do you good,' she said. And all it amounted to was escaping for a few hours from the decayed gentlewomen to the decaying gentry.

In the music room the daughter of the house called Penny was carolling *Das Veilchen* and Klaus Rist was accompanying her on the piano. Her Free French friend Sylvie was closer at hand than necessary to turn over the page. The two young females were united in their enthusiasm for Klaus's musical genius and mesmerised by his physical presence. Not exactly moths around a flame since they were both so plump. They lingered around the piano as though he were something they had been waiting to happen. The yellow patch on the back of his field-grey tunic was the centre of attraction. They were longing to finger it. Colonel Bacon moved about among the guests with the confident air of a proprietor. Winkie and her husband Garnett also made themselves easily available to dispense any explanations that might be needed. After some polite applause Klaus played a Schuman Romance.

I pretended to be hard of hearing in order to get closer to the music and escape the smell of the old woman's bedside. Once she had a drink clutched in her wizened hands she seemed content. Her eyes followed my movements with unquenchable suspicion. The raspberries were all gone. All that was left on the buffet table were stale cakes and Cyprus sherry. As my hostess said, we were all living under wartime restrictions and they were likely to go on for a long time yet.

'Never mind,' she said. 'We make the best of things. Let music open the gates and we can step back into the purlieus of civilisation.'

I swallowed sherry in an effort to make myself more agreeable. I had to find the strength to tell her how nice of her it was to invite me to her party: and to respond sympathetically to polite enquiries. Twice I had to explain I was German and not French. And I was a friend of the Colonel's. Furthermore I had to agree that the Führer was a gangster. A monster. A criminal who should have been hanged. Yes it was a great relief to me personally to know that he was dead. No, I didn't know whether it was safe for me to go back. Yes, I did so love this country and all its hallowed traditions of tolerance and fair-play. Yes, indeed. Garnett Gethin-Wynne was helpful and charming. He rarely raised his voice above a whisper.

'No politics,' he said. 'No worrying about the war. Just for now let's concentrate on putting the dear old certainties back in place.'

His pink bow tie and his ivory cigarette holder signalled his devotion to culture. He moved among his guests urging them to circulate when necessary. Winkie confided in me and in others that she and Garnett just couldn't wait to get back to France. There was a place just outside Nimes where they used to stay before the war. Garnett still had plans to convert a ruined mill into a holiday home when the time was ripe. But when would that be? I didn't know. An unmanageable silence gripped my throat. I tried gin instead of sherry. I had to find the strength to say something or I would be driftwood in this social swim. The thoughts that occurred to me were unhelpful. Whichever side I had been on, my life had always been heading for defeat. I was more of a Prisoner-of-War than that young man romping away on a Schubert Impromptu.

That music meant nothing to me here. If I were to draw any sustenance from cultured traces, distant sighs, borrowed emotions, I had reached that stage of decay when I could do so more successfully with an old gramophone in the solitude of my cell. Here in this country house I was assailed with the prejudices of a rebellious young woman I thought had vanished long ago. Among these tired well-bred people, enjoying their shabby peace, those prejudices returned to fill me with a dangerous malevolence I could barely control. I helped myself to more sherry in the hope that it would help me to listen with more concentrated politeness.

'It doesn't seem so long ago. Last November was it? And yet it seems an age.'

The Colonel was affecting an even more nasal twang to lend additional *sang froid* to his anecdote. He had a group of elderly people in a corner paying him close attention.

'In Mena, you know, by the Pyramids, on the edge of the desert. I had this transport camp. Driving and maintenance and all that. I came within an ace of being shot by one of my own men.'

His shoulders were shaking so that they could assume he regarded it all as a bit of a joke.

'It was the day after poor old Lord Moyne was assassinated, I don't know whether you remember. Jewish terrorists. Just beyond the trees from our camp in fact. All our chaps felt badly about it. That it should have happened so near by. It wasn't our fault. It was none of our business, in fact. But we did feel rather culpable. And most of my chaps were downgraded because of shell shock and nervous troubles. Good chaps but fed up to the teeth with the desert. Anyway a heavy mist came down as I was on my way back from Cairo. It was so bad I decided to walk the last hundred yards or so to the gates. My mind must have been elsewhere and I didn't hear the guard call out "Halt!" I just trudged on through the mist, and the next thing I heard was a bullet whizzing past my ear.'

That was all it amounted to. The gallant Colonel's confrontation with a bullet that did not have his name on it. They pressed closer to him. Here was a war hero they had long waited to admire. Klaus had left the piano. The two young women had led him to a secluded corner of the conservatory. I caught a glimpse of the daughter of the house returning at speed from the kitchen with a dish of raspberries and cream from what I assumed was a secret store. These delicacies were in short supply and reserved for special favourites. The girls leant over him in his basket chair drawn by a curiosity probably more compelling than physical desire. I found myself somewhere to sit and sip my drink and observe. The plump young Penny shivered with pleasure when Klaus allowed his right hand to rest briefly on her thigh. He wasn't good enough for Meg. No one was, and yet I was furious with the girl. No, not with her. With all that petty nationalism and her election fever. The child would spend the rest of her life banging her head against a brick wall. I tried to express my concern to Olwen, but she would have none of it. Meg was so much of herself when young, she said. In any case how could I understand? Among Welsh nonconformists whence after all both she and her husband had sprung idealism was endemic. So what else could she be? And in the end it never did much harm. Look at me, Olwen said, the end product, safely chained to the kitchen sink. What else could we do except laugh together.

I heard a boastful note in Klaus's voice which made me unsympathetic towards him. There was so much cheapness and indignity about. Why had I ever bothered to be sorry for the young man who sounded so pleased with himself, with his mouthful of raspberries. The girls were so attentive he began to make dramatic gestures. He was talking about a farm in a forest, near the Pripet marshes. Both girls were watching him with their mouths open. He began to make dramatic gestures. He put the dish down and pointed to the glass roof with an imaginary gun to his shoulder.

'We came so quietly, he was terrified to see us down in the yard. He was thatching the roof. And chewing a cud of tobacco. It fell out of his mouth. "Hey, old man," Horst said. "How many daughters have you got?" He was joking. Horst was always joking. But that silly peasant was so frightened, that he fell off the roof. It was alright. He didn't hurt. There were thatch bundles under him. He didn't have daughters. But our Oberleutenant was very keen on birds.'

The girls laughed and he looked from one to the other in search of an explanation.

'Men call girls birds,' Penny said. 'Sometimes in this country they do.'

'Real birds,' Klaus said. 'Birds that fly.'

He frowned because a piece of English slang had eluded him.

'Our Oberleutenant was what you call a bird-watcher. And the Pripet marshes are famous for their birds. He was up a tree with his binoculars, and what he saw was a man with two little girls running to hide in the woods. He was a good man, our Oberleutenant. He could tell they were Jews. This peasant had been hiding Jews. But we let them go. And we gave the farmer cigarettes in exchange for cheese. Not long after we were ambushed and the Oberleutenant was shot through the head. I'm sure you two know what it was all about, that war.'

I saw both girls look at each other and resolve to comfort him. What else were they good for? Why else did they put on so much make-up and splash on stinking scent? He might be good enough for them, but not for Meg. Not even as a distraction from that lugubrious Griff Kenyon. She was a precious child and I still longed to wrap her in protective tissues. My glass was empty. I felt a powerful need for more drink. Alcohol was not permitted at the Residential Home For Decayed Gentlewomen. This was a puritanical prohibitive land outside these tiny oases of Ascendancy. As far as I could see at the Rectory sherry was only used for cooking.

The plump Miss Penny Gethin-Wynne was offering Klaus her hand. 'I've got some more music in the nursery.' I heard her say.

'They stored it there while I was away. Shall we go and choose some?' I watched them escape. The young people. Penny, Klaus and Sylvie. He would be offered more than music and what he was offered he would take. They were crossing the frontier into territory unknown to me. Who are all these people in this place? Remnants of a more prosperous past served with sour food by ghostly servants. There was a butler who seemed to me to be covered in a green dust from bald head to boot. The guests are mooching about, waiting for more music, in search of souls they seem to have mislaid, or something more to drink.

I settled opposite a woman in black whom I judged to be an authentic aristocrat: pale, balanced, self-contained, at ease with herself. She was referred to as 'Lady Herbert'. Her fingers twisting the stem of her glass suggested an abiding preoccupation with the confusions of our existence. She was someone I could talk to.

'Never mind,' I said. 'At least we shall all go down together.'

She gazed at me with polite curiosity. My accent had intruded on her daydream, but she wanted me to know it did not disturb her unduly. I liked that. She was someone I could talk to.

'Ruins everywhere,' I said. 'Rubble and ruins. Dust everywhere. We are living on a shattered globe. Don't you think so?'

She smiled at me graciously.

'Never mind,' she said. 'It's all over now. Or will be soon.'

'Ah. But will it?'

Here was an intelligent woman who would enjoy a frank discussion. Echoes of intelligence overheard in Oma's salon.

'All these petty nationalisms rearing their ugly heads. You know my grandmother believed to her dying day that the Austro-Hungarian Empire was the most civilized state the world had ever known. I used to laugh at her. Now I think she was right. And now of course it's too late.'

'We still have the music,' Lady Herbert said. 'From Mozart to Mahler.'

She was being sympathetic and gracious and I admired her for it. I felt I owed it to her to be open and truthful.

'The Americans will throw a cloud of nauseating uniformity all over it, your British Empire. What's left of your world they will turn into commercial colonies and playgrounds. All noise and basic English. Quite horrid. You know I'm relieved I shan't be here to see it.'

Lady Herbert's back straightened and she rose to her feet. Somehow I had offended her.

'I think you are being far too pessimistic,' she said. 'Will you excuse me?'

Unpalatable facts are like unpalatable food. They cause nausea, dizziness and a state of unease The truth was never found in a glass. Rubble and ruin. Dust everywhere. I was quite right. I drew my finger along the arm of my chair and inspected it with undisguised disapproval. They were a stupid lot. They think they've won whereas in reality it is simply that they've lost and don't know it. Why should I keep my mouth shut. Because it never does to know better. Let them go on thinking they know all the answers. Sit tight. Let somebody fill your glass and let that grinning Colonel see that you get back in one piece.

iii

I have been infected with enthusiasm. That is too clinical. And too grudging. For the first time in years I live from day to day in a condition of suppressed excitement. And it's not just my daughter. I abandoned the appearance of a reluctant recruit when I encountered the candidate in the playground waiting for someone to bring the key to the infant's schoolroom. There were men loitering down by the bridge and a ministerial student had gone down to try and coax them to come and listen to the candidate. Llywelyn was enjoying an unexpected moment of repose. With his arms folded he leaned against the school wall and gazed longingly at the ancient church in the trees across the river. I was struck by the pallor of his long face and the unstinting honesty in his eyes. It wasn't because I was a clergyman he murmured how much he would like to spend a few minutes alone in the church. Just long enough to soak up the atmosphere, lick his wounds, be in touch however briefly with the source of power. *We can't win*, he said. *But we have a simple duty to make History relevant to the Here and Now.* In that moment I was captured. I had to accept my share of an honourable burden.

I can barely wait for the call to the next chaotic mission, even on Sunday, when according to the rituals of this pious country all secular electioneering is suspended. My congregation is even less than usual. Sir George and his staff are conspicuous in their absence. Several 'Decayed Gentlewomen' appear to be temporarily indisposed. I am not daunted. Tomorrow I shall drive off in any direction they send me and the landscape once so indifferent to me and so impervious to the progress of events will acquire a magical capacity to pulsate with its own dramatic content. My motorcar sprouts wings. Driving becomes a physical extension of oratory. 'My friends,' I shout as I cut yet another corner, 'dear comrades, consider what is at stake. Exercise your democratic privilege while there is still time....'

In fact I do have my oratorical moments. People gather round and I take off my jacket to show that I am serious. They are curious about my dog-collar and black vest. They think an Anglican clergyman should be on the other side. But should he be? Perhaps I am reverting to my nonconformist roots? In any case to tighten the link between myself and my audience, handful or roomful, I claim to be one of them. The son of a hill farm, or even better a labourer among labourers rolling up his sleeves. I wax lyrical about the smells of the hedgerow and the hay harvest and the beauty of their countryside and how it should all be theirs to enjoy. We have to reawaken our will to live as a distinct people, stand up for ourselves, harness our sleeping pride and learn once again after the weary years of war how to be free men and women in a free country.

Exhortation rolls off my tongue with an ease I never enjoyed before. It feels both dangerous and delightful. Democracy I have discovered is evangelical in its essence. It is the duty of a minister and a priest to exhort his flock, inspire a whole people to organise their social life on the principle of brotherhood, of mutual aid, of equality, of service — these truths are not so much self-evident as intoxicating. When I see open mouths and frowning foreheads, they generate renewed inspiration and vigour rather than obstruct.

I don't know whether Olwen has noticed what is happening to me. She has her own duties and preoccupations. Our days are unusually full and it is often after midnight when I arrive back, and she is already in a deep sleep while I lie awake rehearsing the small triumphs and disasters of the day. It gives her obvious pleasure to see her daughter and her husband taken up with the same enterprise. She is sceptical of course, and even ventures to tease us by declaring that her own sympathies veer towards Labour, and that, in any case, the fortunes of our little country were too closely enmeshed with those of the entire United Kingdom, not to mention the mighty machinations of the United States and Russia, for our puny little efforts to make the slightest impact. Of course, we say, of course. Drops of rain on the floodtide. That does not absolve us from making an effort. I add, once Meg is out of earshot, further consoling reflections about loyalty and the faithful remnant and the melancholy beauty of a Lost Cause. I am pleased to see her smile. Our exertions seem to give extra strength and even a touch of gaiety to a wife and mother who is by nature cheerful and uncomplaining.

'I'm a bit worried about her, Edwin, to be honest with you....'

I am absorbed in the fate of a nation and Olwen is worried about the condition of one old woman in an institution. There were other thoughts it was wiser to refrain from expressing.

'So I've asked him to supper. Griff is taking Meg over to the Roberts's place which is just as well. He says he is absolutely dying for a game of chess with you.'

'Who says?'

'Charles Bacon, of course. Honestly Edwin you are so absent-minded these days. You seem to have gone potty on politics.'

Charles Bacon. Does this mean she has adopted the habit of calling him Charles Bacon instead of Colonel Bacon? Come in,

Charles. How nice of you to call.... I must not pass sarcastic remarks or she will gain the impression that I am jealous. There is wine on the table and I'm sure we haven't bought it.

'Now what about that game of chess?' she said.

She spoke as though it were some kind of treat which I couldn't wait to enjoy. The Colonel tweaked his moustache and rubbed his manicured hands together. My heart sank. I wasn't all that good at the game. I didn't mind so much being beaten by Eryl — or even by Meg. My son Eryl is patient and he laughs at me indulgently when I display my fear of losing and change a move. Chess in my study is a ritual game reserved for the closest members of my family. In any case this evening I was intending to concentrate on one or two new themes for my election speeches. I know the helter-skelter of electioneering is no time to develop fresh concepts on the nature of community and nationhood. All the same one has to make time to condense political philosophy into immediately intelligible phrases that have appeal for ordinary people. Such as, this is your square mile and because it belongs to you, you belong to it. Therefore you have the privilege and the duty to preserve it, to develop it, enrich it and respect it and so forth. It may be little but in an over-crowded and fragmented world among the ruins of the cities and the rubble of unrestricted urban expansion, it becomes ever more precious. How much land does a man need and how much freedom is he entitled to by right and so on? These were all important things to ponder. They needed to be tailored and trimmed into the deftest and most striking phrases that I could memorise and scatter like seed all over our stony constituency. Instead of that we are drifting around the chess table and Olwen is asking whether she ought to light a paraffin lamp to improve the atmosphere. The gallant Colonel holds out his tobacco pouch in her direction. 'With your permission?' 'But of course,' she says. I have the distinct impression of being a prisoner in my own study.

Olwen never showed that much interest in chess before. She hovered about until I had lost my bishop and then she announced she would go and make the coffee. The Colonel looked up from the board to say 'How kind'. And Olwen said, 'Nothing like coffee to clear the brain'. I listened as intently as any spy on the lookout for coded messages, rebuked myself for such absurd suspicions and forcibly focused my attention on my next move.

'I didn't want to bring this up in front of your good lady.'

At first I thought my opponent was mumbling down his pipe in order to break up my concentration.

'I'm afraid our friend the Countess blotted her copybook at the Gethin-Wynnes'.'

Was I supposed to sympathise? He was the one who insisted on taking her there. I stared at the chess board as I tried to fathom the Colonel's motives for taking so much interest in the Countess.

'She got drunk and became quite offensive. She told Lady Herbert her brother had died in order to make the world safe for Joseph Stalin. That may be true but now is not exactly the time to say it. I more or less had to carry her home.'

He tended the bowl of his pipe and squinted at it with the approval of a craftsman pleased with his handiwork.

'Anyway I've made some further enquiries. The fact is, my dear chap, the old bird's got a record. Not so old as that either. A mere fifty-seven. As a matter of interest, is there an age limit of any kind for getting into the Residence?'

He had become more interested in adding to Cecilia von Leiden's dossier than our game of chess. My inclination was to take the game as an excuse for wrapping myself in a cloak of impenetrable silence.

'The fact is, and it gives me no joy to say this, her late lamented spouse was what we call a double-agent. Not the Graf von Leiden of course. I refer to that very suspect Anglo-Irishman Thomas Rupert Clarke. Also known as Theodore St John Gregory and one or two other fancy aliases. Reputed to have visited both sides in the Spanish Civil War on the pretext of being a documentary film maker. First with Falange sympathies and then as Red as Red can be. Not that it did him much good. He was bombed in the Blitz as far as we can gather trying to stitch up a film deal with a Soviet agency. Shall we say killed in mysterious circumstances?'

He was leaning over the table to whisper like a man giving away state secrets and expecting me to be grateful for information I hadn't the slightest wish to hear. Even more than the Countess herself, he was an intruder into my little world which was just recovering enough strength to give out what I would like to consider a still sad music of its own. What was all this about double-agents? And Reds and Blackshirts, Fascists and Communists except a grinding regurgitation of the terror and tragedy of our troubled times? How could we ever make a fresh start while men in glittering uniforms insisted on dragging us back into the very situations we were longing to escape from? Men like the Colonel had a vested interest in a treadmill of public preoccupations. For the sake of politeness I had to say something.

'Who are "We" exactly?' I said.

'Well there are reports....'

He eased himself back in his chair prepared to enlarge on his own importance.

'I have my sources. Chums in the Control Commission I used to help out with transport. And there are other sources, in Whitehall as a matter of fact, that I'm not at liberty to divulge. There are some very curious details. Very curious.'

He waited for me to ask what they were. I declined to oblige and allowed my hand to hover over the board as I considered castling.

'I'm not saying she will cause an international incident exactly, but relatives or persons who claim to be relatives, refugees you might say, in flight from the Russian Zone have filed a complaint and a claim from the Control Commission. I don't know what will come of it, if anything, but they accuse the old girl and her late husband of having absconded with the family silver. Jewels and that sort of thing. Including apparently a crucifix they call the Holy Nürnberg Rood. There's some talk of an investigation. Thought I ought to warn you.'

He waved his pipe like a wand as he bestowed upon me yet another favour. I was to understand that I was in his debt and that it was not too soon for me to ponder how to pay back so many offerings of grace and favour.

'We're not out of the wood yet, are we? Plenty of unfinished business. As I say I don't want to upset your good lady. And we don't want to see your boy sent out to the Far East, do we? If there is anything at all we can do about it.'

It dawned on me then why Olwen was so intent on entertaining this Colonel. Somehow or other he must have given her the impression he had sufficient influence to prevent Eryl from being sent out East on Active Service. There is no limit to the gullibility of mothers where the welfare of their first born is in question. And that cross and those jewels. They were hiding in my old safe in the corner of this room, and if the report were true I could be described as a receiver of stolen goods. I saw myself being drawn and dragged into the investigation: interviewed here in this very study.

Olwen tapped the door to warn us of her approach. She assumed we were absorbed in our game. She was laughing to herself as she pushed in the trolley.

'Sorry I took so long,' Olwen said. 'Believe it or not our coffee grinder had rusted.'

I was expected to join in the merriment.

'Now then Edwin. This is real coffee and it comes to you by courtesy of a certain kindly Colonel.'

I needed to understand why I disliked the man so much. He was our guest and I had an obligation to be generous in thought and deed. More than that as a minister or a priest I was virtually under oath to abjure the gratifications of malice and ill-will. All the same I know that charity without justice is a futile dispersal of goodwill. He was up to something and I had a duty to protect my wife from his manipulations and her own excess of benevolence. Why so much interest in the Countess? I was under the impression that he had taken her up in order to re-launch her in the class of society he imagined to be her birthright. And this musical Prisoner-of-War he had taken under his wing. Olwen had let slip that the boy's grandfather was or had been something like the Burgermeister of Bremerhaven with interests in shipping. Who could have told her that except the Colonel? Transport. That was the key. And those friends in the Control Commission. I sucked at my empty pipe and stared at the chess-board while I assembled the pieces of the Colonel's motivations together.

I had lost the taste for real coffee. I also lost both games of chess. He was much too good for me. This was the way he had whiled away the tedium of his duties in the Middle East and on the Home Front. When he wasn't busy constructing a network of useful connections. This is what they call Post War Reconstruction. The Colonel was resolved to be well placed to profit by it. As the evening wore on he took us increasingly into his confidence. He belonged to the Travellers and he was being put up for an even better club. He was involved with an informal group — not without influence in the Mother of Parliaments — that was dedicated to the speedy economic rehabilitation of the British Zone in Germany. We were to understand that things hadn't changed all that much. Germany was still the most effective bulwark against the Communist menace and it was in our interest to put her back on her feet as soon as possible.

'Mind you, I have to say this, Rector. You may not approve. I've always preferred the Germans to the French. That's how it often is, isn't it? In this wicked world. You prefer your enemies to your friends.'

I found this ridiculous like so many of his pronouncements. Talking about nations as if they were composed of individuals as uniform as a string of sausages. It was unutterably depressing to contemplate that all the power left in the world was in the hands of blinkered oafs encased from head to foot in armour-plated prejudice. Perhaps he could sense he was beginning to get on my nerves? If he could, it did not unduly bother him. Only one more jolly instance of life's continuing musical comedy.

'Good lord, I must be repeating myself,' he said. 'It's time I shuffled off. I have duties to attend to. As my old commanding officer used to say "Who custodes the custodian?"'

This was a high humorous note on which to end the evening. Olwen said she would escort the Colonel to his vehicle in order to fill her lungs with the balmy night air. There was a full moon riding high in the sky and our daughter Meg should be home any minute. She might even walk to the end of the drive to meet her. From the front door I was allowed to overhear his cheerful remarks about the beauty of the peaceful night, and whether that was Jupiter or Venus. Some jealous impulse made me hurry to the kitchen window where I could observe them arrive at the pick-up truck. I lay in wait like a hunter who knows he is liable to be caught in his own trap. There was enough light for me to see him lift her hand to his lips in an elaborate courtly gesture. Then he placed his hands on her shoulders and she allowed them to remain there. Any moment, as occurred so regularly in those novels she was inclined to keep on her side of the bed, his lips would meet hers. This was more than submission. She was guilty of participation. There was absolutely nothing to be gained for our son by going to these ridiculous unseemly lengths. This was something I did not wish to know about let alone watch. I was more hurt than angry that she should subject me to such an humiliation.

The noise of a tractor approaching disturbed them. With astonishing speed Bacon leapt into the driver's seat, and switched on the engine and the lights. The Hendrefor Fordson was trundling up the drive lit with only one small unlawful lamp. Griff was bringing Meg home. I was so relieved I hurried to the front door which was still open, to greet them. Meg was all laughter and excitement. For her life was still glowing with innocence and youthful escapades. At any age, women are unfathomable creatures. They thrive on admiration. They are not necessarily fickle but there is no known formula for anticipating their preferences and judgements.

'Are we breaking the law?' she said. 'The gallant Colonel didn't seem to mind. He was waving at us like long lost friends. He looked ever so pleased with himself. As if he'd just won another war.'

Olwen stepped slowly towards us with both hands clutched behind her back. A model of judicial impartiality.

Meg's smile was a light in the darkness. Something for me to dote on. A man has a daughter to make up for the shortcomings of his wife. Women command the portals of survival of course. More than that. They are the disturbers designed to remind slothful men of the unfathomable mystery of existence.

'I say the most awful things to him, the gallant Colonel,' Meg said. 'He doesn't seem to mind.'

We were her admiring audience. She was important and she had our undivided attention. Election fever was giving her a taste for startling pronouncements.

'"I must be a natural pacifist, Colonel Bacon," I said. "I hate the English but I couldn't bear to kill them. So why should I want to kill anybody else in the whole wide world?"'

'Meg,' Olwen said. 'That was in very poor taste. After all the poor man is English.'

'Bed, everybody! Bed!'

Meg spoke as if she were in charge of the entire operation.

'Three days to go and then three weeks to wait. Why on earth should they take so long to count? Everybody up at the crack of dawn. One last supreme effort.'

'To change the course of history,' Olwen said. 'You mustn't expect too much, you two. It's quite possible you will lose your deposit.'

I could see both Meg and Griff look pale and appalled at such a prospect. To lose was to be lost.

'So don't expect too much,' my wife said.

She was so cool. The very soul of rationality. The mother of all wisdom.

'And then you won't be disappointed.'

iv

I landed with a conclusive thump that pushed the air out of my lungs and I lay there, outside my own door, unable and unwilling to move. This was the end and I didn't particularly mind. If you have tripped over the edge of the world there is nothing you can do about it. You lie at last among the fallen. And there is not a soul to help you. *On your feet, girl! On your feet.* I could hear the squeak of that fat Swiss nanny my mother dismissed for helping herself to a glass of zabaglione. I was upside down on the branch and I was enjoying it and telling her not to worry. My feet were in the air and my hair flowing with the water and the clouds of the sky mixed with the pebbles on the bed of the river. I told Fraulein Steiner not to worry. She squawked. *We are here to worry about each other, child. It is our business.* I wanted to laugh then and I wouldn't mind laughing now but you need your breath to laugh. There was nobody who would choose to worry about me, and why should they? I giggled on the floor as I searched my mind for those who would choose to help me, who would run to put me back on my feet. The joke is, they themselves are all among the fallen.

Those evil children. They left the metal box so that I should trip over it. They went to the trouble of dragging it to my end of the gloomy corridor. Malice aforethought. Little thugs in the making. Recruits for some vicious new political force already rising from the ruins. Rats in the ashes. I refuse to lie down and die just to please them. One must survive. Wise Phyllis leaned over me as I lay on the beach in Lleyn like a landed porpoise, her eyes enlarged by the urgency of her wisdom as well as the thick lens of her rimless spectacles. *One must survive. I'm a survivor. You must survive.* It was an article of faith and I had to accept it with that immense emphasis on the verb 'survive'. The cottage was damp. The fuel exhausted. Hardly any food left. All I could do was lie on the deserted beach, stare at the heaving grey metallic seascape and hope to fall asleep and not wake up. In any case I was weak and the sloping pebbled beach was difficult to walk on. I had lost my stick and could not go on. My husband had been killed in the bombing. I had a ration book but no money. What else was I to do?

It's our duty to carry on. I looked up and tried to take strength from the warmth of her proselytising zeal. This was Phyllis Williams, the vet's wife. Eager and childless. He had no time for me, but Phyllis had spent a holiday in Garmisch-Partenkirchen, and claimed to appreciate the charms of German culture. Her brother Geraint said he could save my bacon. He was a lawyer, plump and amiable and short of breath with a microscopic interest in social and political machinations. *You must call yourself 'Countess' Mrs Clarke... My father always used to say a title was worth five hundred a year.* Phyllis loved her brother more than her husband and called him a fat old cynic. They used to laugh together. She would hoot and he would wheeze as they contemplated yet another local variant of the universal affliction of human folly. He steered me into this place which conforms to the gospel of survival so ardently preached by his sister. He died with sweets in his mouth, reading a book in the shade of his favourite tree.... Sub *tegmine fagi*, his sister quoted solemnly. *Dear Geraint died with a smile on his face. You see, he knew I would carry on.* Phyllis conducted her existence on the basis of a conviction that with proper care she might well live for ever. As luck had it she was crushed and stamped on by a mad stallion. I was not able to attend her funeral, and yet thinking about her strengthened my resolve to get back on my feet.

Cries and whispers in the corridor. 'She's drunk. She is! It's a disgrace. Bringing our institution into disrepute you could call it. The foreigner! The woman has no idea how to behave....'

I couldn't quite identify individual voices. There were three or four inmates clustered together, clutching the tops of their cardigans against their throats. Not one of them made a move to help me. They were too busy working themselves up into a lather of indignation. Such useless barren female fools.

'Lying on the floor too drunk to get up. Filthy foreigner. Did you ever hear of such a thing? Just look at her. It's a disgrace and it has to be reported.'

Four ageing females with just one miserable little thought to share between their shrinking skulls. I wouldn't accept their help even if they offered it. I would survive if only to spite them. I could make an effort to reach up to the door handle and drag myself as far as the mat alongside my bed.

I was bruised and stiff. It seemed I took hours to undress and get into bed. A night disturbed by aches and pains and even more painful dreams. All concerned with escape and pursuit. Over icy mountains and through dark forests. I was the little girl who sat on the end of the sledge and kept the wolves at bay with a broken whip. I escape by train. My first husband lies dead on the luggage rack wrapped in a Turkish carpet and it is my duty to spirit him over the frontier for a decent burial. He is too heavy to move. Heavier than that old green safe in the corner of the Rector's study which I couldn't move an inch. I was afraid to wake up and discover myself transformed into that purposeful dead weight I so much dreaded. I had to go on living in order to prevent a swarm of bat-like harpies invading my little room and rummaging through my things with their steel teeth. As long as I was conscious I could drive them off with my stick.

Mid-morning a miracle happened. Like a shaft of sunlight, a shower of gold, Meg came to visit me. She expressed satisfying indignation at my condition. I attempted stoic endurance and an understanding smile.

'They make me furious. That lodge family,' Meg said. 'Jingo-istic Labour of the worst kind. You've no idea. And as for the regiment of monstrous old women....'

She spoke from the depths of her electioneering experience. I wondered how she could take the time from coping with the world's affairs to visit an old woman like me. I murmured an attempt at ironic appreciation.

'I don't know how you could spare the time, Meg my dear, to visit an old nuisance like me. I'm not even on the electoral register.'

'It's over,' she said. 'And of course it isn't. The votes are cast. And there are three weeks to wait for the declaration. It's unbearable. Worse than an exam. Of course the election isn't an end in itself. I know we can't expect to win. On the other hand I don't know what we'll do if we make a poor showing. I can't bear to think of us losing our deposit. That's the nightmare. I mean, what kind of a people are we?'

It wouldn't be for me to tell her even if I knew. I was a foreigner. A stranger. An enemy alien or at best a neutral. All the same I had my impressions and they were not altogether favourable. My grandmother's Viennese culture meant nothing here. The only Austrian they had ever heard of was Adolph Hitler. As far as this outlandish corner of the earth was concerned Sigmund Freud and Alfred Loos and Gustav Mahler might as well never have existed. All the same this dear girl and her mother were agents of survival. They brought light into my darkness. Just to look at her face revived my spirits. Even when she was frowning and her lips pouted in a captivating sulk.

'Klaus says Germany is the most beautiful country in the world, and you can't blame a whole people for the evil deeds of a bunch of political gangsters. He's right, isn't he?'

Was this the reason for her visit? Her concern for my welfare was genuine enough. Like her concern for the well-being of the entire human race. It seemed to me what she most wanted at the moment was to know what I thought of Klaus Wilhelm Rist. Anything I said would tend to sound like a warning and to a young person, so generous and so impulsive, nothing would be more counter-productive.

'You oughtn't to be stuck in this place, you know. That's the truth of the matter.'

It was easy for her to be forthright. She was making me stir uncomfortably in my bed. I should make the effort to get up. Perhaps I could ask her to make me a cup of tea? Why should the thought prevent me from speaking? Strange how an excess of affection can inhibit one's natural impulses. Why shouldn't I ask her? She would be glad to do it. I do not ask because I want to hear her make the offer.

'Those horrible old women. They're no good for anything except to make a person's life a misery. You're much too young to be stuck in a place like this. You may not be as strong as you should be, but you are young in heart. Would you like a cup of tea?'

As I expected it came like a phrase of music, soft and beguiling. 'Oh my dear, would you be so kind.'

I would like to have said it was worth being indisposed in order to be waited upon by such an exquisite servitor, but I judged it wiser not to. When she turned and bent her head to smile at me it was like a benediction and I was free to become a foolish fond old woman.

'Germany is going to be such a terrifying problem,' she said. 'The entire economy has ceased to function. Klaus says next winter there will be nothing but hunger, cold, epidemics, starvation. He doesn't say much but you can see he's worried stiff. Griff wants to go to Italy to join in the refugee work. Klaus says Germany will be far far worse than anything we can imagine. He's likely to be right, don't you think?'

Klaus says this and Griff says that. It was so easy to imagine them both vying for her attention. That would give her a certain power. It was important for her to learn how to use it. If she were too trusting and innocent she would be more likely to suffer. These were the eternal truths I had to find a way of imparting to her without giving offence. She should know that beauty in itself is a dangerous inheritance. I am not doubting their sincerity, but they are male. The elemental power of the life force is so much more apparent to those safely outside its orbit. Lying in bed with the warmth of her cup of tea between my hands I still need to take into account my own affection for this girl and the strange desire to see her small again, so that I could spend my day fondling and stroking her. Unrestricted love can always give birth to some fresh perversion. And possessive love is incapable of innocence. As I am witness to my own emotions I swear I intend nothing but the best for this child.

'Klaus thinks you ought to go back to Germany. The need there is so great.'

She was studying me in my narrow bed with such wide-eyed

innocence. I had to contain the pain in my chest. Her voice was a child's voice uncovering the extent of my guilt and my deception. I had spun too many tales by the fire in the Rectory kitchen. I felt a sudden nostalgia for the blackout and every single wartime restriction. Those evening classes in the school where we sat close together around the stove to enjoy the residual heat from the afternoon cookery class. How old was she when it all began? Now the dangerous flux returns. And we are free to move and be moved, and she becomes the first agent of a force that will drive me out of the only refuge left to me in a hostile world.

'The blackness of that place.'

She leaned closer to hear me whispering.

'I can't go back to it. I would rather destroy myself.'

She looked cross with me.

'You can't say that,' she said. 'It's still such a wonderful country. Klaus was telling us how big the fields are without silly little hedges everywhere. He doesn't like walls and hedges.'

How painful the truth is. All the effort I have put in since I came here to avoid facing it. How hard I have struggled to bury any unwelcome fact that would disturb the new image I had created for myself. What kind of Peace is it that opens old wounds and puts my whole life once again in question?

'There's so much you could do there. It's your duty to be there.'

I have to have a child like this to lecture me about my duty. She should be listening to me. She should be drinking in the wisdom I distil from years of bitter experience. I am a woman of fifty-seven who has lived and breathed for so long on a knife edge; who has kept her balance by a precarious combination of rationality and a base instinct for survival. Would she ever keep still and listen for long enough to learn and understand?

'We could come with you,' she said.

'"We"? Who's "We"?'

It was an effort merely to ask the question.

'Griff and me. Klaus too. He is making an appeal for repatriation on compassionate grounds. So have half the men in the camp, he says. I think he has a little bit of influence with the Colonel. Anyway it's time to be moving. It's time to find new ways of dealing with things as they come up.'

'You can't be everywhere, child. You can't do everything.'

I had to try and smile and look like a qualified exponent of common sense. It disturbed me to see such an untried girl being so restless. These were still terrible times. The urge to destroy was still abroad like a pestilence for which there is no known antidote. She was quivering around my little room like a caged angel.

'I can tell you this, if we lose our deposit I shan't want to go on living in this stupid little country any more. I can tell you that much.'

I managed to go on smiling at her and shaking my head like a person of goodwill lost for the right words. Their parliamentary election meant nothing to me. But she was the most precious thing in my circumscribed existence. If I lost her I would drown in a tide of despair.

FIVE

i

My enthusiasm for the cause evaporated the moment the campaign was over. I knew our efforts would be overwhelmed by a tidal wave of votes from all points of the compass, and in three weeks the results would be announced with the finality of a prison sentence. Somehow I had managed to live with my feet a few inches above ground level and when I came down to earth it was a bruising bump. What kind of world did I think I was living in as I dashed from one corner of the county to another with a burning coal on my tongue? This corner of a green paradise was in danger and I was one of the team elected to save it. I woke up and the burning coal turned into a cool thermometer which assured me that I was a nonentity, and all the sound and the fury of my eloquence amounted to less than nothing.

It was dispiriting to become aware of the indifference and the inertia of our esteemed electorate; of the waste of time and effort trying to woo them and win their votes. Indifference and inertia. With a chilling degree of accuracy I was able to measure the very same qualities in my own character. In any case we were too small and the world was too big. We were a race of serfs and the serf has no real urge to set himself free or be set free. He has an affection for the chains around his feet. So why should he change? Llewelyn, our candidate, was an impassioned and impossible idealist made to be brushed aside by party machines and the business of politics. Even if by a miracle he were to be elected he would be trodden underfoot in the stuffy corridors of the mother of parliaments. His brand of saintly patriotism was too much for our breed to swallow. He was too good for them and by the same token too good for us. We were destined to lose our deposit because we didn't have the energy or the desire to save it.

'Look at these,' Olwen said. 'Just look at them!'

A heap of American magazines. Not the kind of reading matter I would choose to buy. They came in all their garish splendour by courtesy of our gallant Colonel. It was the pictures my wife was thrusting under my nose, as though they were proof that she was so much wiser than me. Somehow these pictures excused her irregular behaviour.

'We have to face these facts, Edwin,' she said. 'We can't go on living like ostriches with our heads in the sand.'

I am the ostrich. The Colonel is one of a band of gallant knights who at least tried to ride through the burning forest to attack the wicked giant in his grim fortress to rescue rows of damsels and fair matrons in distress.

Why were their legs so wide apart, those shrivelled corpses hanging on the barbed wire? She wants me to concentrate on pictures of smashed-up concentration camps. Fat men and women in soiled uniforms being forced to carry more skeletons, more naked corpses. German civilians being compelled to witness stacks of starved corpses. They pass by with handkerchiefs pressed more to their noses than their eyes. I too am looking until I am numb. This was the world I escaped from and I can't bear to come back to. For how long had I slept through this earthquake? Sitting in the Rectory kitchen I could still feel the tremors around me. There was too much to look at. Too much to take in. Normality had never existed. My wife marches about banging the kitchen utensils and I sit at the table, a frozen nonentity staring at pictures.

There are endless pictures of devastated cities. What is left of the scraps of authority that once belonged to my sacerdotal office? I can absolve nobody and nothing. Bremen is a waste land licked by a black river. The ruins of Nürnberg stretch over two pages like a bloated corpse being eaten by blind worms. There is no noise of explosion, but the centre of Cologne has become a black and white catastrophe. Broken bridges sag and sink into water that has lost the ability to flow. Railway tracks bend and buckle into the ground like a shower of arrows aimed at the devils in hell.

What have we got to say to each other? In some way does she hold me responsible for this horror? All my failure, my fault. I serve a creed that is meant to contain if not tame the basic savagery of the human race. I am paid to keep things on an even keel. This is evidence of evil organised on a massive scale. And what did I ever do to combat it? That is what she is thinking, and all I can summon up in feeble self-defence is a whine of reproach: are you any better? We have shared a milk and water mixture of liberal Christianity and Fabian socialism, just as we share our bed and board. What good are our prayers? Nothing more than systematic sighs and groans. I shall never see those stacked corpses arise to be clothed in white raiment. Babylon the great is fallen, fallen, and become the habitation of devils. These were the events of the end of a war and a climax of destruction and life crawls on. Not for these. Not for any of these. I am left to feel guilt of exemption and I can only wait to join them in their burning pit because they have taken away any hope of heaven.

What am I supposed to do? What am I supposed to think? *And God saw that the wickedness of man was great on the earth and that every imagination of the thoughts of his heart was only evil continually....* Does this mean there must be a deluge at the end of every epoch? My wife is looking at me expectantly, but what am I to say? There is an illusion of safety in silence. Unspeakable pictures. I can only move out of their sight and out of her sight without saying anything. I take my bicycle out of the coach-house. She can assume I am engaged in parish visiting while I head for where I am least likely to encounter people. If only I could return to the haunts of my youth, listen to the grasshopper in the ferns and hear the corncrake rasping in the long grass where it rears its young.

Olwen says I idealise my peasant past. Why shouldn't I? Consciousness has become a penance. It forbids us these attempts to climb back into the skin of a previous self. Old memories are proscribed. They have ceased to be trace elements of eternity. So what am I going to say in my sermons? Only beg for pardon. Sunday after Sunday the distance, the separation between the crow's nest of a pulpit to the sea of empty pews

The haunts of my youth. Home from college
the station where the late spring merges into e
life seemed a promise of perfection. Every lar
green expansion of hedges and a familiar wor
The fields of childhood are unchanged shapes
the stream below the farm-track is designed to
It still shelters a moorhen and her brood. As
narrow crossroads you catch your first breatht
the homestead nestling under the hill. In the
house your brother has already planted potatoes
the rows are as straight as his back and his pride
for my birthday as always a boiled egg with my

The smell of new-mown hay. The fine disti
mowing the sap-driven grasses of middle June
hardened stems of mid July. My brother is in cha
kingdom and I am there to do his bidding. The
as the cart load gets higher and the long days an
dawn to dusk. But I never felt freer than wher
empty cart holding the reins and cantering dowr
for yet another load. In those moments I was th
little world and the horse in jingling harness my 1
I recall the shock I felt the winter before last whe
spat into the fire and announced the day of the 1
He had never liked horses since the day a lumber
had trampled over the corns of his left foot. H
second-hand Fordson tractor showed how willingl
in the mechanisation of human existence.

Hard labour. This is what I need. The antidote t
oppression of too much thought. Down at Hendre
welcome my help in the harvest. Off with coat an
dog-collar. Roll up sleeves and work until the
rivulets down your back. Harden these soft hand:
bleeding blisters. A farm labourer among farm
Prisoners-of-War, without any function other than
his bit to the social harmony that makes the harv

oration. Emlyn Parry will be glad to see me. And so will Nell
wife. And I shall enjoy the smell of her giant rice-pudding
king quietly in the wall oven. The world renews its savour in
ple country habits.
ready some of them are drinking oatmeal water in the
dow of the tall hedge. They do not hear me approaching down
grassy lane but I can hear the teasing that can turn to taunting
asily on these occasions. I recognise an adenoidal voice thick
h hints and nudges.
What will you do then, Griff Kenyon? Eh? You've got to do
ething, good fellow. You can't have a Jerry pinching your
t girl. Dammit all. I'm sorry to tell you I've seen them with
ir arms around each other. Aye. Yes I have. That's what you
see, for being a conchie....'
snivelling laugh. Dic Moch mab Meri Ann Clebran — Dick
son of Mary Ann Telltale — so what else can you expect?
at sly insinuating voice and that wet smile designed to assure
ry candidate in sight of his vote. I can't see Griff's response.
e hedge is too thick. I grip the handlebars of my bicycle, as
l as a rabbit mesmerised by a stoat.
I don't know what her old man would say if he knew. Old man
fore his time too, if you ask me. Dried up with dry as dust
mons and always clearing his throat. But it's not right, is it?
rson's daughter not supposed to go flirting around the parish.
hat's the world coming to? It's not a nice thing to see a girl
ing around with bare legs on a bicycle.'
No response from Griff. It must be agony and yet he's putting
with it. I admire his restraint. I must get back home and check
at that girl has been up to. I keep telling her mother it's time
e kept her on a tighter rein. It's up to the mother surely to show
r daughter the way. Teach her to exercise the immemorial
licacies of feminine self-control. Lead her along the path a
tuous girl should follow. I have expressed this opinion in one
ay or another for the last four years and what response do I get?
eg is a very intelligent girl. She is perfectly capable of looking after
rself. I have complete faith in her judgement. That's what I get.

Behind these confident pronouncements what is she really saying? Meg is just like me. Independent and very intelligent. She is my daughter. My one and only successor and I don't see why she should suffer the stifling incarcerations I have had to put up with all my life. Particularly my married life. Who would marry a curate? And end up struggling to keep up appearances in a large comfortless draughty Rectory? Things unspoken. Olwen prides herself on never giving way to a whine or a whinge. But I can read the signs that pass like cloud shadows over her face. What little help she gets and how everything except work and worry is rationed in wartime. She is a woman with academic qualifications and I should never forget the sacrifice she made in marrying me. It is true she has been a devoted mother, an efficient housekeeper and a responsible wife — at least until this Colonel Bacon thrust himself and his perquisites into the inconspicuous but satisfactory course of our existence.

So what am I going to say when I get back? *This has got to stop!* That sort of thing. Bring down my fist on the kitchen table and roar out *I'll have no more of it!* And that applies not only to Meg dashing about with bare legs on her bicycle, but to Olwen and her musical comedy Colonel. *He's banned from these premises! Do you hear me?!* This is the Rectory and I am the Rector and I will have some respect shown to my authority. You must give all those perks and bonuses and fringe benefits back to where they belong. That cantonment of aliens, manned by aliens, planted in my parish, in the very heart of our territory. It is my decision and my decree that you shall have no more to do with him or with them.

When I arrive at the Rectory, I put my bicycle away in the coach-house, avoid the kitchen and make my way through the front door to the silent refuge of my study.

ii

I could not resist taking hold of Olwen's hand. I wanted her know how much she meant to me. It was a small hand, hardened and even scarred from too much housework, and my flow of sympathy and affection increased as I held it in my own. There was no one in the world I wanted more to know what was passing through my mind, with the possible exception of her daughter. However I could tell Olwen things that would be difficult if not impossible for a young girl to understand. That was the difference.

'To think I stood as close to the creature as we are to those women.'

Under her direction three members of the Women's Guild were decorating the area around the altar rail with free-standing flower arrangements. Olwen held her head to one side. She was smiling to show that she was pleased with their handiwork.

'I often think if only I had done something. That one day. That one chance. How many million lives would have been saved.'

I had to dramatise the whole business in order to gain her attention. She used to be so ready to listen to my stories. Somehow or other since the war in Europe had come to an end, whenever I started reminiscing, she seemed to have other things on her mind. Her son might be sent to the Far East. This election business had certainly upset her family life. And perhaps the Colonel was paying her too much attention. Whatever happened it was important, supremely important, for me to hold on to her friendship and her sympathy. Otherwise to whom else could I turn?

'He was such an evil genius and they were always presenting him with flowers. You should have seen the way families competed about who would present him with flowers. It was so uncharacteristic, so undignified. The pushing and the shoving. I was well-born but I wasn't pretty enough. There were cameras about of course. They chose one of the von Borsig girls. They knew the Führer liked to be photographed with pretty girls. It was all so false and it went down so well with the public. Ever since I've thought what a chance was lost. I even dream about it still.'

'A chance for what, Cecilia?'

Olwen raised her fingers and the red and white roses were moved closer to one another.

'A grenade in the flowers. Or a knife. That sort of thing. I don't know. A suicide bomb. Might have killed a handful of people. But if he'd have been killed, back there in '36, how many millions of lives would have been saved?'

She was looking at me with more curiosity than sympathy. She could see no point in my fruitless speculations. That was the difference between us. An unbridgeable cultural gulf. Assassination was a process outside the scope of her imagination. In my background it was a political fact of life. She withdrew her hand from mine, ostensibly to make more signals to the women by the altar. The scale of events were so frighteningly large. Beyond the range of her comfortable world. How could she compute the crimes against humanity, humanity had so willingly committed against itself? She was wondering how much I had been deranged by bombardments and heaps of rotting corpses. Over was not yet over. There are peculiar silent torments reserved for survivors.

'Well he's dead and gone now,' Olwen said. 'Thank goodness.'

She was being honest and simple and irredeemably complacent: but I still loved her. What else could I hold on to? All the same I still needed to make a case in my own defence. At night I saw the Führer's staring eyes ordering my enemies to close in on me. There is always an element of truth in my dreams. Unless I took a new initiative it would only be a short time before they destroyed me. I had to command Olwen's undivided attention and bind her closer to me.

'Ah, but is he?'

'Of course he is. He destroyed your poor country and then he destroyed himself.'

'His ghost is still stalking the world.'

I clasped my arms around myself as if struck by a sudden chill.

'Sometimes I can feel it. All this talk about post-war this and post-war that. He'll be there at every conference. Every meeting.

Because power is the power to destroy. He'll be there laying down the seeds of even more ghastly scenes of destruction.'

'Oh Cecilia. You shouldn't say such things.'

I was making her uncomfortable instead of winning her support. These flowers were in preparation for a wedding. A happy occasion. A local event. A soldier on leave was to be married to the widowed post-mistress's eldest daughter and Olwen was presiding benevolently over the village celebrations. Who better? It was all supposed to be lovely. Simple rituals to reflect the goodness of simple hearts. Is it she who has persuaded the Colonel to allow Klaus Rist to play the organ? Let harmony prevail. The Colonel makes jokes and Olwen seems to enjoy them so much more than the Rector does. If there was an harmonious blacksmith why not an harmonious Colonel? What? He is as ever, much taken with his own wit. From me, I sense, he has begun to distance himself. No doubt because I behaved badly at the Gethin-Wynnes'. I am not useful to him. He would prefer Olwen to take less notice of me too. I am in his power. That is more troubling. There is menace underneath that surface amiability. He has authority and he wants to exercise it. And he has connections in the Control Commission and in the Foreign Office in London, and he wants me to know it. Such immunity as I enjoy, I am to understand, depends increasingly on his goodwill. I lean closer to Olwen so that I can mutter in her ear.

'I am a liar, my dear. And I am a thief.'

Where else better to confess than in a church? Perhaps I should have spoken more loudly. Once the words were out the burden would fall off my back and even my arthritis would be less painful. Olwen had concern for my reputation. Whispers carry in an empty church. The women at the altar were turning their heads appearing anxious to hear more. I should try and demonstrate an aristocratic disdain for what common folk might want to hear. For a parson's wife in this provincial democracy it was different. Here there was some importance attached to what ordinary people might think or say. Olwen was kind enough to take my arm and lead me out along a path between the oldest tombs where I could speak more freely.

'I was never Mrs Clarke,' I said. 'We were never married.'

It was so easy to unburden myself in the peace of the graveyard. These were confessions beyond the usual warm confidences that most women readily exchanged. The dead were such sympathetic witnesses.

'He was a bit of a rogue really, Tom Clarke. A charming scoundrel. But how was I to know it? I was trapped and he seemed to offer a way of escape.'

It was vital that Olwen of all people should understand why it was impossible for me ever to go back to Germany. She was paying me close attention. All I could do was present the unpleasant facts in all their crudeness and rely on her sympathetic understanding to make them acceptable to her daughter.

'If you can imagine my world as it was then. For me Schoenfeld was a prison. For Tom it was a most marvellous film location. A mediaeval castle complete with legends. One of the early Counts had hurled his wife through a window. That sort of thing. He seemed to have money but in fact he had none. What little he had were grants from the Ministry of Propaganda. Goebbels' money. To make acceptable images of the new Germany for foreign consumption. What did he see in me? A childless middle-aged woman with an ancient title, a ghastly mother-in-law and a homosexual husband. Does that shock you?'

Of course it did. It is difficult to be honest and to present oneself in a favourable light. The facts are so shameful. Was I a victim; or the architect of my own undoing? I searched Olwen's face for guidance and I suddenly saw myself as I was then, a woman on the threshold of middle-age, vexed and even tormented by a vague and yet overpowering sense of being left behind, of being lost in a wilderness of time.

'You can't imagine the ridiculous pretence and the secret miseries. For my mother-in-law nothing mattered except the façade, and for fifteen years I did all I could to keep it up. Until Tom came along. He was almost ten years my junior but he made me laugh. He made the scales fall away from my eyes. Or maybe I exchanged one set of scales for another. Pink ones for grey?'

I made little gestures with my fingers to illustrate what an objective, even lighthearted, view I was able to take of the whole sorry business. The bloodiest battles in history should have obliterated my trivial misadventures. And yet here I was sitting on a gravestone forcing myself to bring them up again.

'How did you get away?'

There was such innocence in that enquiry and her voice was so youthful it could have been her daughter speaking. It was comforting to be together in this ivy-covered corner of the graveyard. This was true friendship. She was entitled to nothing less than total honesty and I had to summon up all my strength to speak.

'No heroics, my dear. Nothing anti-Nazi. Just a sequence of petty deceptions. Manfred had an ex-S.A. youth living virtually in hiding in a cabin in one of our forests. I found him repulsive. Manfred loved him. He was in serious danger. Something political. Manfred wanted to get him out of the country. Tom would arrange it. For money of course. That was where the second deception started.'

Confessing wasn't easy. A form of humiliation. I sat on the edge of a tomb and pressed the palms of my hands against the warm surface. I could claim it was all part of the human condition. Look how one impulse can ruin a whole existence and another rescue it. How do we survive our choices? The answer is we don't. A whole civilisation has collapsed while this lichen under my finger expanded its modest space on this stone. The only truth is written in the dust.

'My mother-in-law was on a visit to relatives in Silesia. It was the perfect opportunity. I filled two suitcases with jewels. Were they mine or were they hers? As I saw it I had paid for them with fifteen years of unremitting misery. We can always find excuses. We dropped the bully-boy off in Zurich as promised. It was as simple as that. So simple and so clever. We were so pleased with ourselves, you have no idea. The trouble was we could never go back. I knew it at the time of course. What I didn't know was that we were doomed to wander the face of the earth, and discover how little we had to say to each other.'

I stiffened my back in order to avoid slumping into self-pity. It would be so easy and so comfortable to do that. Tom Clarke was dead and I could blame him for everything. Cheating and lying and betrayal were the tools of his trade, but he never deceived me more than I deceived myself. That was the plain truth.

'He claimed so many connections in Wardour Street and in Elstree and in Ealing. All those places. When they found out he had nothing to offer except himself it was amazing how quickly they dropped him. He was ready to try anything. Desperation I suppose. He tried to set up something for Germany in the United States. A propaganda film you could call it. It will be so subtle, he said. Too subtle, they said. Don't you realize we're Jewish? He was such a fool. We were left with nothing but those dreadful Aunts in Streatham. When it started the war raised his hopes. All sorts of new opportunities, he said. Then he began to complain that things were moving too fast for him. Too much chopping and changing. He wanted to move to Ireland. Then he parked me away in that cottage in Lleyn. The ends of the earth it seemed than. I suppose it was the best thing that ever happened to me. Do you know it wasn't until he was killed that I found out the cottage belonged to an actress he was having an affair with. Poor Tom.'

'Poor Tom, indeed. He sounds an absolute rotter.'

Her sudden outburst of indignation made me laugh.

'No really. It is awful when you come to think of it,' she said. 'Men stalking around the place looking for women to take advantage of. It isn't right, is it?'

She saw me smiling and it was easy for us to laugh together.

'Remember how you used to tell me to write my memoirs? Now you know why I never did.'

'Oh I don't know,' she said. 'There's nothing more interesting than the truth.'

'And nothing more terrible. No more stories,' I said. 'My past is rolled up and finished with. Like the black-out. I've come to a conclusion, my dear. Here and now. In this lovely graveyard. I have no right to blame anyone or anything except myself. Not Fate. Not History. Not even Adolf Hitler. I was always a wilful little beastie. That's what my Scottish nanny used to call me. *Cecilia. You are a wilful little beastie.* And now all I will and all I want is to be buried here. In this lovely graveyard. Do you think that is still possible?'

I wanted to ask her to respect the secrets of the confessional. There was no need to ask. She was a woman whose chief strength in life was her fund of goodwill. She took both my hands in hers and I knew my secrets were as safe with her as were the jewels in her husband's study.

iii

Union Jacks and Red Dragons dangled every other above the tables spread around the Memorial Hall. The best of both worlds. Out of rations and illicit farm produce a feast had been conjured up and eaten up. One thing about rationing: it gave people a good appetite. On the top table Irwyn y Gof and Dilys Post looked rigidly happy. Dilys was conscious of the chaplet of small flowers balanced on her thick black hair. Irwyn's forage cap was still stuck in the shoulder strap of his khaki tunic. Most of our conscripts had been scattered to the four corners of the earth. Irwyn's gentle boast was that he had never been posted further abroad than Wootton Basset. He was popular and she was popular and this was an occasion for rejoicing. I had said as much bilingually. That more or less completed my official function. Everyone was considerate, respectful, polite. This was how they wished to be seen and it was as close as it could be to what they were. I had no grounds for complaint about the people of my parish. All the Nonconformists were unfailingly co-operative. If a population tends to be sheeplike it is hardly appropriate for the shepherd to complain. We are humble and we are awesomely respectable. And what is so wrong with that?

The meal was almost over. There was music now, supplied by three German Prisoners-of-War: piano, fiddle and accordion. My parishioners were fascinated by the novelty of the occasion. The mother of the bride was looking around expectantly and wondering what on earth might happen next. Dancing was no part of her tradition. It could happen. Something new. Something different. The Colonel was moving about in the background, conspicuously inconspicuous in his glamorous uniform. He gave the proceedings the stamp of official approval direct from the War Office. Sheep may safely graze in pastures supervised by a Providence that had established permanent headquarters in Whitehall. If the message passed down from above suggested dancing to a new tune, a habit of obedience would make this assembly quick to learn. Olwen was intent on spreading the new gospel of gaiety. A merry heart maketh a cheerful face. *At least the war is over, Edwin. Here anyway. People have a right to be happy and rejoice.* Who was I to disagree with her? All the same I had an inclination to distance myself from the festivities. I removed my melancholy presence on the pretext of going outside to smoke my pipe.

I sat on the stone bench facing the War Memorial. *To the glory of God and in ever living memory of those who gave their lives for King and Country in the Great War 1914-1918 —* death in both languages. Thirteen went out from this parish and never came back. Record the names with pride and history will let the rest of us off. All I can remember are the faces of boys in the uniform in the lowest ranks displayed with the same unsmiling smudgy sadness in the columns of local papers. More names to come when this war comes to its official end. An American general has threatened Japan with two million tons of bombs in 1946. A matter of time he says. What isn't? Pray God my son's name won't be carved on that stone. His last letter complained of heat and mosquitoes and the waters of the Mediterranean like a sticky hot bath and the sand scorching the soles of his feet. The staff quarters of the hospital were troubled with a plague of fleas. He had made a plan to drain the land behind the hospital but he was having trouble getting approval to put it into effect. Local problems. Local customs. Arabs not always easy to deal with. Slippery, says Eryl. Forthright, my son. Cool, firm, practical, hard working. The man to get things done, more like my brother than me, I suppose. The only person I could really talk to these days. Man to man. Father to son.

'As soon as the harvest is over, I'm going.'

Griff Kenyon was standing in front of me pushing the gravel with the toe of his shoe. He has drifted towards me because I am the only person he can talk to. In his Sunday best an unwanted guest. He is never at ease with himself. That powerful frame. Those restless blue eyes and the fair hair perpetually falling over his forehead.

'I'll go wherever they send me. China. The Far East. I haven't suffered enough.'

It came from the depth of his being. He was a troubled soul, my prospective son-in-law. Too ready to torment himself. It was my business to provide him with a minimum of consolation.

'You mustn't court suffering, Griff,' I said. 'It will come to you soon enough. What about the corn harvest at Hendrefor? How will they manage without you?'

'They'll manage. Plenty of Prisoners-of-War. They've got Klaus and he gets on well with the Colonel. They can get as many men as they like. Cheap labour. The local lads won't like it. That's the way it is these days.'

Through the open doors of the hall we could hear excited chatter as feet began to shuffle to the throb of unfamiliar music. This was a strange wedding. The first perhaps of a new era in the history of my parish. Hardly any alcohol except for Cyprus sherry in the trifle, and whatever the mighty Colonel Bacon had contrived to contribute. The volume of noise suggested some form of growing intoxication. Puritan restrictions and restraints were being trodden underfoot to music. Soon the Lord of Misrule would peer in through the stained glass windows with nods and winks and vulgar signs of encouragement. More laughter, raised voices, occasional cheering. This must be one of the new freedoms we had been fighting for. Any minute now they would emerge through the open doors like prisoners set free and dance off in search of a destiny.

'I know I'm not wanted. I don't see why I should be here at all. They made me come. Meg and Mrs Pritchard. I knew I wouldn't be wanted. They said if Klaus was coming I should come. I knew it would be a mistake.'

'I thought you and Klaus were friends. I thought he was a man you could talk to.'

'He thinks I'm a fool. He says I haven't heard the news that God is dead. He laughs at everything I believe in.'

'Oh dear.'

The tone was wrong. I'm not his priest but I am his friend. I should not have tried to sound as cool and as impartial as an academic in a seminar. Griff reacted as though he had been stung.

'He has no respect for women. He has no respect for anything. And that's because he's got no principles.'

'I'm sorry to hear that. As I say I thought he was someone intelligent you could talk to. Weren't you explaining the *cynghaneddion* to him? That sort of thing.'

'Crossword puzzles. A way of stringing together petty bourgeois platitudes. That's what he calls them. That's how he is. Always trying to drive a wedge between me and the things I love and admire.'

'What do you mean, no respect for women?'

This had to be a matter of some concern to me. After all it was common knowledge that they were both my daughter's admirers, and as far as I know, in spite of Dick Pig and his insinuations, the friendship was generally approved of. I had taken comfort from the spectacle of their comradeship: the girl, the Prisoner-of-War, and the conscientious objector. I took it to be a promise of better things to come — more civilised behaviour. There again Olwen frequently reassured me by saying what an intelligent girl

Meg was and how we had every reason to have faith in her judgement.

'Klaus says women are naturally promiscuous. All of them he says. Patriarchal societies were set up not only to safeguard property but to keep women in check. The only real affection they have is for their offspring and maybe occasionally for each other. So that makes feeble nonsense of that romantic mush I've been writing he says. I was stupid enough to try to translate things for him. He thinks he's so clever. He says I should go back to science and not write another line of verse until I'm past thirty.'

He could repeat these lessons by rote and it was clear every single proposition hurt. What could I say to comfort him? He had taken his stand as a conscientious objector and it was up to him to see to his own defences. It was a sign of weakness if the German could penetrate them so easily and leave him like this, repeating his casual censures as if they were holy writ. It was time he went away. Time for him to discover fresh perspectives; acquire a more solid basis for his attachments and preoccupations. I would be doing him no service by ministering to an inclination to self-pity. He has to find a way to rise above all this. Otherwise he will sink into that state of complacent mediocrity where I seem to spend the best part of my time.

Meg came out of the hall to look for him. Her cheeks were flushed and it was easy enough to see why people spoke of her as the Rector's beautiful daughter: that was no reason for me to display unguarded or unqualified approval. She was smiling and determined as usual. She took hold of Griff's sleeve and shook it.

'Come on,' she said. 'We are trying to teach them a Breton dance. You know, where the dancers link little fingers and shuffle and snake along in a line. You've seen my mother do it. It's not the right music of course, but we might invent something new! That would be fun. You come too, Tada. There's nothing to it. It's so easy.'

I waved away her enticements. Griff Kenyon was more her problem than mine. It would be a relief to be rid of the young man and his over-active conscience. Not so simple of course to get rid of my own, while I squat between a War Memorial and a wedding. That is the way of it. We are marooned on this earth to feed our lives on a perpetual diet of alternating hope and despair. Even here, so comfortably far away from the zones of cataclysm. What use is Mr Llywelyn's vision of a glowing future or my own unwritten history of this parish's glorious past if all that the present can offer is unrelenting mediocrity? Why should I be plagued with resentment? And even worse eaten up with some nameless envy?

'Edwin!'

My wife stood in the open doorway calling my name. Something between a summons and an invitation. Her voice was a vital part of the mutual society, help and comfort that went with holy matrimony. I should know. I had recited the words often enough. She was designed and intended as an image of cheerfulness breaking through. Except for the shadow of the ubiquitous Colonel moving behind her. That man was never still. Always prowling about with his knees bent and his brown boots gleaming.

'Edwin. I nearly let the cat out of the bag.'

'What cat?'

She was standing in front of me smiling motherly encouragement.

'Cecilia's jewels in your safe in the study. I nearly told Charles Bacon about them. It almost slipped out. What's the matter with you? You look as though the world was coming to an end.'

'Isn't it?'

Why should we bother about this self-important Colonel. Just what authority was invested in a military tailor's dummy? Who did he think he was? The Occupying Power? The governor of a conquered province?

'I think I've persuaded him to leave the poor old thing alone. And stop talking about her as an enemy alien. Anyway, he's put in for a transfer.'

I refrained from sarcastic comment. All the same it was cheering news. I could look forward to seeing the back of him.

'He says his special expertise is in Transport not prison camps. Ever since he was a boy, he says, he has been fascinated by railway systems. And they will be the key to quick recovery in Europe. He's champing at the bit, he says. The trick is to get in on the ground floor. There's a fortune to be made and all that sort of thing. He needs to be in London, he says. That's where the contacts are. He would just love the challenge of working in the Transport Section of the Control Commission. There's nothing more he can do being stuck out here. You've got to be at the centre of influence to get at the heart of things.'

The Gospel according to Bacon. She sat beside me clasping her hands on her knees like someone experienced in bringing comfort to the bereaved and sick at heart.

'We have to admit it, our experience is so limited,' Olwen said. 'When it comes to facing the things that are going on in the world. We are better off than most you could say but as a society we have lost the habit of independence. I mean independence of thought is a form of sovereignty and we lost that so long ago. We've been resigned to living on the nursery slopes. Those who want to climb the heights have to go away. It's become part of the nature of things and part of our nature. We've forfeited a vital inner resource you might say. That's why I think we ought to give Labour a chance. At least we would be more accurately represented.'

She hadn't voted for us. I never asked her. And this I took to be her way of telling me. She gave her vote to that Labour prat in spite of what Meg and Griff and I were saying and doing. One vote less and one more betrayal.

'I admire your Mr Llywelyn. I really do. A solid block of integrity and concern. But you've said yourself he was never designed for the rough and tumble of Westminster politics. That seems to be one of the more bitter lessons of recent history. Beware of idealists. They'll only get you into deeper trouble.'

She was expecting me to agree with her. She intended this as a sweet phase of reconciliation in the sunlight. I was to accept that everything that she did was for the best.

'Now listen, Edwin. The trick is to move before they move. To pounce before they pounce. We must get her out before she's thrown out. The poor old thing needs protection. If it goes on like this her life will be nothing more than one long nightmare. A cottage at Cae Helen has fallen vacant. You could use your influence and get her in there. I know she would absolutely love it. All she wants is to spend the last years of her life in peace. Late autumn peace, she calls it. The poor old thing.'

'Out of the question.'

It was all I could manage to mumble through the resentment rising in my gorge.

'Why? Why is it?'

I stared at her with the baleful eye of a basilisk.

'Why do you attach yourself with such ease to foreigners and strangers?'

'What's the matter with you?'

'Talk about inner resources. Where have yours disappeared to I wonder?'

'Edwin! All I asked was a simple question. You sound so resentful. What has the poor woman done to displease you?'

It was incredible that she could adopt such a pose of being worldly wise and yet be so unaware of a local difficulty right under her nose.

'If I were seen for one moment to be giving that German woman preferential treatment, all hell would be let loose. Can't you see that? There are men coming back from the war. Soon the trickle will become a flood. There are local families already without proper housing. That pair in there!'

I pointed histrionically at the open doors of the Memorial Hall. The cheerful noise proclaimed the continuing success of the dancing and rejoicing.

'Where do you think that young couple is going to live and sleep and bring up a family? In the back kitchen behind the Post Office? Wake up, woman, and take a close look at reality.'

'Edwin. There's no need to be so unpleasant.'

'You can be sorry for everybody and anybody. So can I. But

as far as my duty is concerned I can't attach any more importance to a so-called countess than to the most humble farm labourer in my parish. Understand that.'

iv

He was grinning down at me from the gable door of the hayloft like a gargoyle on the top of a drainpipe. So pleased with himself, so impudent and familiar. This so called musical genius with his concupiscent grin and that faun-like affecting power on his narrow cheeks: and that wispy moustache that makes him look younger rather than older, reminding me, against my will, of sepia portraits in those padded albums at Schoenfeld. He was up in the heights his hands planted confidently on his field grey knees as he leaned forward to greet an inferior creature confined to ground level.

'Did she have a word with you, Countess?'

He was brimming over with confidence, ready even to give me advice. He had shed that odd reluctance to speak German. In a matter of weeks he had travelled so far, the war was years behind him.

He was all eagerness for the future that belonged to him far more than it could ever belong to me. I was cross with myself for ever having wasted sympathy on the creature. Even worse, nursing kitchen maid fantasies of a romantic attachment between him, totally unworthy as he was, and my wonderful Meg.

'We don't belong here,' he said. 'How can they ever accept us? This isn't our proper place. We don't fit.'

How much had he seen or heard of my humiliation at the Gethin-Wynnes'? His presumption was unbearable. I saw his hand alight again on that plump girl's thigh. He had intruded into my little world and now he was trying to push himself further into it: interfering with my nest, threatening the remnant of a warm wartime shelter that I still cherished more than life itself.

'She's a great girl though, isn't she?'

Thrusting his thoughts at me, intruding on my private space.

'I've heard from my people, they are safe and well. They were hiding you might say in Uberlingen, that little village by the lake. Untouched by the war it seems. My grandfather is very ill. They need me. My father needs my help with the business. I have made my appeal for repatriation on compassionate grounds. The Colonel says he will help. He is interested in Communications. Life must go on, Countess.'

His elation disturbed and depressed me. What life goes on? And what was the connection with Meg's high-flown concern for refugees and rehabilitation and whatever she chose to call it? An excuse to follow this boy to Germany? The young are capable of anything. So where was that milk and water conscientious objector that he should allow it? A stupid old woman has no means to predict the random processes of sexual attraction among the young. No control whatsoever over a new species emerging out of the wartime twilight into the harsh glare of this so-called peace.

'You have work to do,' I said. 'Don't let me detain you.'

I made my way across the stony farmhouse towards the house. It is not easy on such a surface to proceed with formal dignity. I did not look back. What I needed was a weapon: something to obliterate the difference in power between infirm old age and youthful male vigour. My will was perfectly capable of being stronger than his. He was laughing at me. I would wipe the smile off his face. Shooting a wild irresponsible fool is no worse than shooting a wild duck. Whichever direction I look my position is too vulnerable. I must take steps to defend myself. No one else will.

Nell Parry met me in the open doorway. Her sleeves were rolled up, her pinafore stained with calf-meal. She carried a bucket in each hand and was slow to put them down. There wasn't much welcome in her lopsided smile. I raised my stick to point at the date carved under the coat of arms above the doorway.

'Time honoured,' I said. 'Fleur-de-lis, and the lion rampant. A chevron between gold stars.'

'Nothing to do with me,' she said. 'Won't you come in? Can I offer you a cup of tea?'

The woman was constrained by Celtic courtesies and I took advantage of them. She had no real wish to see me. When I visited with Olwen we vied with each other in singing the praises of a kitchen where the salted hams hung from the rafters and the stone floor barely had time to dry before being scrubbed again. I watched her sinewy arm lower the black kettle on to the fire. This too would have been incorporated into my private Welsh paradise if I had not been so free with my criticisms about her precious conscientious objector. I had been too full of my own pert observations to observe how much the barren farm wife doted on him as an only son. The peculiar torment of folly is to be incapable of forgetting it.

'I must be one of the few people in the world who are sorry to see it coming to an end.'

I imagined it was quite a tactful thing to say. The war had pinned down Griff Kenyon in Hendrefor which was what she wanted. Now the restrictions and barriers were being pulled down the gullible creature was more than ready to fly the nest. I wanted her to understand her world and mine were beset with the same malignant uncertainties. She looked at me over her shoulder with suspicion disguised as polite incomprehension.

'Nobody wants to see our boys sent to the Far East,' she said.

Two uncomprehending females in the quiet of a farm kitchen. Outside some kind of a lull in the prolonged hay harvest. I close my eyes and the silence of the house makes me ever more acutely aware of the miracle that brought my unquiet restless existence to rest in this paradisical parish: this oasis of green peace in a world obsessed with the raging terrors of war. I cannot express any of this to a woman who sits at the centre of it as if she were chained to a post. I might say something trite enough for her to understand that would bring her some comfort. Such as that stuff about the moving finger having written moving on, and how when people snatch at the illusion of being free to go where they like, their problem will be to know where to go.

'My dear Mrs Parry,' I said. 'I am here to do business.'

I made an effort to be excessively amiable. I pointed at the shotgun between the dresser and the corner cupboard.

'You told me it was never loaded. Now can I buy it from you?'

I may have sounded playful; making a daring proposition.

'For this ring,' I said.

I held up a knuckled finger so that her eyes could take in the indestructible brilliance of the sapphire. I wanted her to be mesmerised by the reflected light and the desire to possess it, to stare at it until its value had eclipsed any sentimental attachment to the gun.

'It was my father's,' she said. 'Emlyn has no use for it. Griff used it once to shoot rabbits. He said there was something wrong with the sights.'

There was something wrong with his sight. Could he not see himself being replaced by a German soldier in Meg's affections? Should I urge this woman to encourage the fellow to stand up for himself? Not that any man in this world ever listened to an older woman who gave in to his every whim. Her head seemed to waver on her shoulders as she struggled to make up her mind.

'What good is it to you?'

I was ready with my answer.

'A deterrent,' I said. 'It's what a woman needs when she lives alone. You understand?'

I detected the first trace of sympathy in the way she looked at me. She was the local equivalent of a simple peasant woman after all; hardworking and put upon, with nothing to say to the absurd social pretensions of the decayed gentlewomen. She understood my threatened position: that I lived virtually under siege.

'There was an old maid in our village at home,' I said. 'She kept her father's hat and his gun in the hallway of her little house to warn off possible intruders.'

I smiled but Nell Parry was not amused. Perhaps the predicament of a nervous woman was too close to her heart. At any rate it seemed to incline her towards accepting my offer.

'How would you get it there? Where you wanted it?'

'Suppose you wrapped it in a sack and left it in the outhouse at the end of the lane. Put it in the manger behind the beam where the old gravedigger hanged himself. No one ever goes there. And so I shall collect it after dark.'

An intense anxiety was gathering in her face. I thought she was pondering my proposal before rejecting it. Her stare was fixed beyond me. Griff Kenyon stood in the doorway, his face as bloodless as a ghost's. He was muttering to himself. Mrs Parry understood what he was saying. He was slow to take in my presence.

'I've killed him,' he was saying. 'I've killed him.'

Nell Parry could not bear to watch his agony. She moved towards him, her arms outstretched to comfort him.

'My boy,' she said. 'My boy.'

He shook his head and turned away.

'Get a doctor,' he said. 'He's bleeding. Get a doctor. He'll bleed to death.'

He was distraught. As I struggled to my feet I saw him stumble up the stone steps to the stable loft. He locked the door before Nell Parry could reach him. Her sympathy would do nothing to assuage his anguish. We stood together in the middle of the yard listening to him whimper. He was locked in his torment and we could do nothing about it. We were as helpless and as isolated as he was. If the loft burst into flames now before our eyes all we could do would be stand and watch it burn.

V

'It must have been an accident,' Olwen said. 'You know what it's like Edwin, on farms I mean. They can so easily happen.'

A brawl in a haybarn could hardly be called an accident, theologically speaking, any more than the creation of the world. But if that was what my wife chose to believe, it was my business to agree with her. Anything that should not have happened is best described as an accident. An unfortunate accident rather than an untoward incident. These fine distinctions are an essential ingredient of the cement that holds the social order in place. They permitted us to travel together with unruffled calm on the service bus, since I had exhausted my petrol ration in my fruitless electioneering, in the bonds of Wales and the cause of the estimable A.W. Llywelyn.

The cherished landscape we see through the window is so overwhelmingly peaceful, it would be wrong to allow such a quiet corner of the world to be unsettled with rumours of untoward and ugly events. That is the way to look at it. There is a sense in which all civilised living is a ceremony of concealment. As a man of peace and a quondam man of God, my business is to prevent an unfortunate accident being transformed into a criminal offence.

'People have no idea how easily these things can happen.'

My wife was muttering her litany to herself. It hardly mattered whether or not I heard her above the growl of the bus's engine in low gear. Her words were a part of a world view we shared, and that meant we could draw comfort and reassurance from the sharing.

'Life on the farm can appear so idyllic from a distance. In reality it's tough and rough and bloody. After all we only rear animals to slaughter them. On a farm you can't afford to be sentimental. It's only when you move away it begins to look picturesque and the further away you go the more romantic it looks.'

Sitting in the bus and looking through the window. Unless we can keep our instincts and desires firmly under control we are nothing better than an inferior species of animal ourselves. This business of falling in love: what is it except the excuse we need to unleash our animal desires? The affairs of the young disturb the settled order of things. They force us against our will to re-examine our own emotional record. These boys so recently become men were reputed to be friends. Not David and Jonathan perhaps, but two young men from different countries and different cultures who could communicate with each other on a decent intellectual level: on a rational basis. They had so much in common, it seemed to me, so much they could share, the north German and the north Walian. Whatever their friendship it couldn't stand the strain of sharing an affection for my daughter. So what had sexual passion got to do with love, the moment you subject it to rigorous analysis?

The service bus removed us from one parish into the confines of another and yet another. It was comforting to contemplate the consolations of landscape. Differences in contour can bring out subtle differences in character even among an ancient homogeneous people. Dry walls that run up mountain slopes like pretty decorations were put in place by hardened hands. Like the slate they handle, quarrymen can display a brittle dourness that distinguishes them from their amiable slowfooted kindred toiling on a low-lying land. So I like to think. You can distinguish the seamen, liable to sing lustily from the back seats of their chapels, from the shepherds who prefer to converse on the hillside with their dogs. To write an adequate history of a parish requires a man to penetrate more deeply into the nature of existence, and he should be able to do this without any damage to the sensitive surface of his personal feelings. There is an urgent need for this work to begin. It should be done before the engines of communication accelerate and obliterate for ever the delectable patterns of local differences.

'Edwin! Wake up! We are here.'

I hastened to descend from the noisy vibrating bus with all the dignity I could muster. There was an agreeable smile fixed on my face in case I should overlook the duty of greeting any parishioner I might chance to encounter. Olwen was always better at taking people in and distinguishing between them. She strides ahead of me as we make our way up the steep hill to the Cottage Hospital. She turns around to admire the view and wait for her husband to catch her up.

'Do they know...?'

I breathed deeply to prepare myself for the coming encounter with the Matron. My son Eryl was quite a favourite with her and he was bold to the point of familiarity.

'Matron Mars, one of the stars,' he would say, and she enjoyed it. With me she was always more formal. Eryl took after his mother. He had a way with people.

'She knows all she needs to know,' Olwen said. 'Charles Bacon has seen to that. And Matron has an inbuilt respect for those set in authority over us.'

I tried to look impartial and amused. The affair was being hushed up as I understood it for Griff Kenyon's benefit. No doubt Colonel Bacon had other motives for rendering such benevolent assistance. Olwen seemed determine to raise my spirits.

'"A cottage loaf in charge of a Cottage Hospital,"' she said.

She was quoting one of our son Eryl's humorous remarks.

'He thought that extremely funny.'

'He' of course would be the gallant Colonel. And I was supposed to be grateful for his help. Which of course I was. It was all a very messy business, disturbing the even tenor of our ways and giving me no peace at all to settle down to writing my parish history. A mass of information circulating one man's brain cells is of no possible benefit to the rest of humanity. Matron Mars Hughes appeared from nowhere as we waited in the small reception area. A large woman with a small head, arrayed in a military style uniform that could have been of her own devising. Like her surroundings she was scrubbed and polished. A faint air of disinfectant and chloroform clung to her clothing.

'I always tell my girls, a nurse should never be nosey. She should remember at all times to act as a hostess in the wards and treat all visitors as guests, and of course be scrupulously clean. You know, Rector, old Doctor Denzil used to say, "Welsh girls make the best nurses." "Yes indeed, Doctor," I used to say. "Everyone's heard of Florence Nightingale, but who ever mentions Betty Cadwaladr?" And do you know what answer I used to get? "Matron, virtue is its own reward."'

Her mouth puckered in a small smile and her piercing glance compelled me to smile back in homage to the memory of the redoubtable Doctor Denzil.

'A member of your family has arrived before you,' the Matron said. 'Made for medicine, you know, just like her brother. "What makes a good nurse?" she asked me. Such a thoughtful young person. "Hard work," I said. "Self-denial and a constant subordination of her own will." Am I right, Rector?'

Of course she was right. And what was Meg doing here at least twelve miles from home, and how did she get here? Flying on a bicycle through four different parishes. Flying in the face of established order.

'Such a clever girl. I never knew she spoke German. Such a help to us. It contributes so much to the comfort of a patient to be able to converse freely in his own language.'

The private ward she said was on the second floor. A charming room where the patient could lie in bed and admire the view overlooking the estuary. Everywhere windows were wide open. Matron Mars tramped ahead of us smiling the tight smile of approval of a presiding deity that surveys all her handiwork and finds it good. I looked around for some sign of my daughter. Even the seagulls wheeling outside the windows looked clean enough for the matron's approval. The door of the private ward was open and there was the German Prisoner-of-War looking better than I had ever seen him. Sitting up in bed with his right shoulder artistically bandaged. The moustache was gone. He looked comfortable and well looked after and pleased with himself. The matron was pleased with him too.

'The wound is healing beautifully,' she said. 'Our patient is well on the way to a full recovery.'

In the doorway she confided in me in a Welsh undertone.

'Such a charming young man. Such good manners. And his English is very good. A great favourite with the nurses.'

And with my daughter. The matron gave the patient a small wave of approval before moving backwards with as light a step as a ballroom dancer. She passed the French window that opened to a rose garden on the terrace. It was there I saw Meg leaning on the stone balustrade apparently admiring the view, and looking very much at home. In the private ward the German raised his hands in a gesture of submission.

'You have nothing to worry about,' he said. 'So I am very glad to see you.'

I waited for Olwen to say something. It wasn't my place to speak first. Instead she merely nodded her greeting and made for the terrace. I saw Meg turn to register her mother's approach. It seemed to me her attitude was defiant. If there was to be a confrontation she was confident of holding her own. I seemed to be the only one demonstrating unease, even though I had made the journey in the interest of reconciliation. I was here to reassure both parties to a dispute for which I was in no way responsible.

'I provoked him,' Klaus Rist said. 'I may as well admit it. He hurled his pitchfork straight at me. I dodged, but I was not quick enough. It struck me in the shoulder. It was bad. But I am not making any complaint.'

'I am very sorry,' I said.

There was no real necessity for me to apologise. I must have done it from force of habit. Apologising for my own existence as well as for Griff Kenyon's lapse into near homicide. The German was shaking with suppressed laughter before he winced with pain.

'Excuse me, but it is comic,' he said. 'If you look at it this way. I have come unscratched through the war in order to be speared by a mad pacifist!'

He looked so pleased with himself. I suppose it could be said he had come through: to survive is to triumph. He was ready to flourish and bloom in this private ward. He assumed his visitors would be delighted with whatever it occurred to him to utter from the sanctuary of a hospital bed.

'He's a nice enough chap. As a matter of fact I like him. But he has one layer of skin less than anybody else. So it is too easy to hurt him, you understand. He is not protected. And then he is so innocent. Like a baby. And so gullible. You can make him believe anything.'

The matron claimed he was a great favourite: I found him verging on the repulsive. Why should Meg be so anxious to be near him? I turned away because I could not bear to look at him. His face was glowing with the pleasure he took in his own brilliance.

'He has to understand it is a different world now, we have to live in. It is no use dwelling in the past, I tell him. We have to make our own future, I say. These unhealthy fantasies and guilt-ridden feelings will be no help at all....'

He assumed that I was standing at the foot of his bed in order to share the pleasure of his recovery as well as his pronouncements. To stand and listen was my penance. My daughter was responsible for his condition and in the scheme of things I was responsible for my daughter. Her presence in the rose garden filled him with a sense of well-being and filled me with foreboding. Colonel Bacon had decreed we were all to carry on as though nothing untoward had happened, so my wife informed me. Therefore I was to ignore all the alarming transformations that were taking place. This Prisoner-of-War could sit up in bed primed with all the answers and the confidence to put them into practice. We are told he and his kind have lost the war: and yet here he is propped up and smiling as though the future were in his hands. A new race of positive people are taking over the direction of the universe. Preachers and parsons will be relegated to the ranks of blind and unquestioning obedience.

The voice of Colonel Bacon ballooned up the stairway. I saw him march down the corridor, slapping his polished leggings with his cane before pointing it through the open door at the patient who was making it plain how very pleased he was to see his camp commandant.

'There he is!' the Colonel said. 'Lucky devil. Some people have all the luck, don't they Padre? It's homeward bound for you, young man. In a matter of days I may say rather than weeks. If you behave yourself. And by that I mean a quick and smart recovery. Isn't that so, Padre?'

The young German was clenching both his fists and shaking them. The Colonel insisted that I should look just as pleased as they both were: join in a celebration as if our team had won. I was trapped between two specimens of an alien species. They had so much in common, including a blissful incomprehension of all the qualms and concerns that dominated my waking and my sleeping hours. If they chanced to glance in my direction all they saw was a dog collar and a black vest.

Colonel Bacon held my arm and led me down the corridor for a private conference. I had to restrain myself from shaking my arm free of his grip.

'You know in its quiet way, Rector, your parish is quite a little storm centre.'

In spite of his patronising smile he was expecting some show of gratitude. I was to understand that in the interest of my flock and my family, he had exerted his influence in several directions. Was it for the sake of peace and quiet, or in the interest of my daughter's good name, that I was now engaged in the laborious mental exercise of framing an adequate expression of thanks that would retain the vestiges of dignified independence and not lurch over into an exchange of fulsome compliments?

'The fact is, Rector, the hounds are closing in. The old girl will have to be extradited. I don't know the details of the due processes of law any more than I expect you do. The thing is, these von Leidens have pull. A lot more pull than you think. Friends high up in the Control Commission and they seem hell-bent on getting their hands on her. And more importantly I suppose on those blessed jewels, wherever she's hiding them.'

The Colonel sighed heavily. An extra weight of responsibility was descending on his shoulders.

'It's none of our business, of course, in one manner of speaking. And yet in every other you could say it jolly well is.'

He gave me time to say something. There was nothing I could think of saying that did not appear to me to make matters worse. I had no special brief on behalf of the Countess but I could not bear the prospect of sinking deeper into this man's jovial clutches.

'Anyway, old chap, I felt I had to warn you.'

Here again he was doing me a favour. This gave him a

prescriptive right to address me as 'old chap'. How many favours would accumulate before he took it upon himself to call me Edwin.

'I see the ladies are here. Can I offer you all a lift back to your own dear little parish?'

vi

I have always refused to be afraid of the dark. Even when that awful Nanny Frenssen shut me up in a cupboard for refusing to eat cold spinach. That must have been a vital step in my education. As I see it the phases of our improbable existence are bound together by swathes of darkness that are the true sources of comfort. It is out of these that we conjure up those odd tremors we mostly refer to as happiness. That night when Tom Clarke and I hid in the luggage van we were concealed by pitch dark, and I loved him more than ever before; or afterwards. That is enough of weaving myths out of transitory experience. Memoirs indeed. Let someone else do it. Action is all that matters. When you stop moving you are dead. The trick is not to be a burden or a nuisance to anybody except yourself.

'A gun is not much use without ammunition.'

I was gratified to see Letitia Hughes-White racked with a curiosity that drove her habitual asthmatic wheeze into abeyance. She had seen me carry the shotgun to my room. In her effort to find out what I proposed to do with it, she was prepared to go as far as engage in polite conversation. Odd to recall the effort I made to befriend this woman in the early days. She had a superficial charm she was prepared to exercise when it suited her. The Rector in his innocence imagined two well-born relics would at least have genealogy in common. I may have been inclined at that time to flourish the Almanac de Gotha: to confuse my pursuers rather than impress new acquaintances. One wall of Letitia Hughes-White's room was entirely taken up by a framed decorative family tree. Very fanciful. A brightly coloured root proclaimed her descent from Amlawdd Wledig. This allowed the silly woman the claim of being related to King Arthur. 'Isn't it absurd,' I said. 'The von Leidens claim descent from Scipio Africanus.' An unsuccessful pleasantry.

'It looks pretty,' I said. 'These days a woman shouldn't go anywhere without a gun.'

'What will you do with it?'

'Knock intruders over the head,' I said. I was prepared to demonstrate. Letitia went into one of her controlled asthmatic spasms and withdrew from the field. It was an empty triumph. She had made a serious point. I groped my way in the dark down the Hendrefor farm lane to remedy the deficiency. To save the battery and in order not to draw attention to my night patrol I refrained from using my little torch. I had all the time in the world to move carefully between the shadows and the starlight. My ancestors were nocturnal animals. The dark offered comfort and security. Only the daylight was dangerous. This isn't the same as roaming the forest at night with the gamekeeper's children but the stars are the same, and at least I am doing something and my spirit is raised with the sharp taste of adventure.

There were boxes of cartridges on the shelf above the bran chest in the storeroom next to the stable. I congratulated myself when I noticed them. They were no use to anyone but they were precious to me. I had been forewarned and I would be forearmed. In the time of the breaking of the nations human beings are herded like cattle from one corner of the map to another. I shall not allow that to happen in my case. I shall continue to exercise my will until I drop. This is my chosen resting ground. Here I shall live and here I shall lie. Long ago I extracted a promise from the Rector of a burial plot. That is the way landscape comes to life and soil becomes sacred. It is quite foreign to my nature but in times like these one can only survive by the continuous exercise of cunning.

I overreached myself and the loose box of cartridges fell into the bran chest that the lazy farmer had left open. I was furious with my own clumsiness. My fingers pushed about as I picked out the cartridges one by one and stuffed them into my overcoat pockets. My adventure was degenerating into a ridiculous enterprise. I was still rummaging in the chest when I was caught, a guilty thief, in the light of the powerful torch. I blurted out in my own defence.

'I am quite prepared to pay for the damage.'

'Countess.'

It was only the conscientious objector. I regretted speaking in such an abject fashion. His spartan quarters were above the stable. No doubt I had interrupted his hair-shirt meditations. The girl had said something about Griff keeping a record of his own weaknesses in order to dismantle his pride. She was always ready to spring to his defence. It was difficult to have patience with such adolescent emotional prattle. If you were a devotee of doing right, life should be simpler and not more complex. I took the offensive.

'Your rival has made a complete recovery,' I said. 'I'm told he looks fitter than ever.'

'I am very glad,' he said.

I felt I heard a pious note in his voice and it irritated me. I might have been caught red-handed but I was not prepared to listen to mealy-mouthed sanctimoniousness.

'You should have killed him,' I said. 'While you were at it.'

I saw his head lower in the shadow of the torch. He was meditating my proposition.

'I would rather kill myself,' he said.

'That is rubbish. The people you love you should protect. Otherwise you have no right to love them. You should be living by yourself somewhere. Like a hermit in a cave. Living on grasshoppers and wild honey.'

'I've thought about that,' he said.

'You know as well as I do that fellow will ruin her. You should have finished him off.'

He was shaking his head, stubborn in his misery.

'You deny your origin,' I said.

It was the kind of lecture I had been aching to deliver to this muscular wretch.

'You are a man,' I said. 'You have inherited the strength of a man. You should use it. You should use your strength to defend all you hold dear. You can't deny the truth of the origin of the species. You must fight to hold your own. You must fight to survive. You must fight. What else are you good for?'

'That sounds very like National Socialist doctrine.'

He spoke mildly enough but I was outraged. I raised my stick.

'How dare you! Just because I am a German. How dare you associate me with that vermin.'

Outside in the yard there was a noise like a cow in distress. Nell Parry was calling out in the dark. Perturbed no doubt that some harm was coming to her pseudo-son. I had no patience with these people. My escapade was exposed. My plan was ruined. I would march away with my few cartridges and offer no explanation for my presence. I moved as quickly as I could out of range of their incomprehensible chatter. I could not wait to hear their voices fade in the distance.

'Don't you come near this place again!'

Nell Parry's voice rose to a screech as she determined that I should hear her.

'Never again, do you hear! Or I'll have the law on you for trespass.'

I was nothing but an old woman shuffling along a dark lane. A bag of bones. Nobody gives a damn whether I live or die. Except myself of course. I had all the reasons any human being could assemble in favour of making a spectacular exit.

SIX

i

Typical of A.W. Llywelyn. He chooses to sit on the edge of the most uncomfortable chair in my study. It is only there to hide the safe of the erstwhile Gwynedd Farmers' Bank, which Olwen considers unsightly. He sits there oblivious of his own comfort with the light of unquenchable optimism on his emaciated face. He has finished at the bottom of the poll, and yet he is still capable of introducing a note of triumph into his husky voice.

'We must battle on,' he said. 'We must never give up.'

Newspapers described it briefly as a disastrous result. To read was to be forced to admit the lamentable truth. The Labour victor went out of his way to compare us to Jonah's castor oil tree. We were a temporary phenomenon withered and wiped out over night. He wanted his electorate to know how familiar he was with his Bible. In the face of it all this man Llywelyn could speak like one who wins and not a candidate who has lost his deposit.

'We must never lose heart,' he was saying. 'Never. I can tell you honestly, Mr Pritchard, this was an experience I never sought. But I can tell you now, I shall treasure it for ever. It taught me so much. And it brought me into contact with such a band of brothers. And of sisters. Such a noble and unselfish band of supporters and dedicated workers. And an unseen army of well-wishers. How many times on the doorstep was I greeted with, "You next time, Mr Llywelyn bach."'

He was a man who could derive encouragement and comfort from anything and anybody. I had only to look at his volunteer chauffeur sitting by the door to confirm this. A plump contented young man happily twiddling his thumbs. Probably the last of the small band of nonconformist theological students exempt from military service who had seized the occasion to make more noise than they would otherwise have dared to. His aunt had told me the boy loved politics. When the time was ripe he would slip out of the pulpit and join a party that would get him into parliament. I sensed my own cynicism like a bad taste in the mouth.

'What we need to do, if I may dare say so, is to make ourselves worthier of the vision we share,' A.W. Llywelyn said.

The man was intolerably idealistic. And yet, against my sober judgement, my spirits were raised, at least temporarily in his company. This was strange. I admired and even envied, his exultation. There was a light in his eyes that suggested he saw beyond what he was looking at.

'We must never lose our affection for the common people. Or our concern for their well-being. I am more convinced than ever that the hungry sheep have an absolute right to look up and be fed.'

There was a smile on his face that made me begin to feel uneasy. He was about to ask me to do something: impose yet another impossible task on my shoulders.

'What we have to do is discover a way of addressing them more directly. We must find a way into their hearts.'

An odd sort of task for an Anglican parson in a nonconformist country, inured to the weekly penance of addressing empty pews in an ill-heated church.

A.W.'s eyes were gleaming as eagerly as a sheepdog's. I knew in my heart I could not share his belief in the innate goodness and wisdom of the people. It had never existed. It was for that very reason I had broken away from my nonconformist roots at the very outset of my inglorious career. I could not stomach the prospect of my material welfare being dependent on the goodwill and charity of congregations made up of an assortment of peasants and proletarians with a sprinkling of self-righteous shopkeepers. To admit as much in the presence of this man was shaming enough. There had to be even more deplorable short-comings lurking under such a surface scum of superficial snobbery.

'This is not facile optimism....'

He looked as though he were about to take his leave. I was

ashamed to feel a certain relief. His presence was a strain because it imposed a constant pressure of painful self-analysis.

'The way I see it, we have to leave a space in our lives for Providence to operate. That sounds ridiculous, but it is as near as I can get to saying what I feel. You know the sort of thing, Rector. "Though he slay me, yet will I trust in him."'

His simple honesty took me by the throat. That had been a verse my mother would quote in her last illness in a way that used to bring tears to my eyes. What use were tears? A.W. Llywelyn was on his feet and looking round my study.

'You must write it,' he said. 'That history of the parish. You really must. For the sake of the inheritance, Mr Pritchard. So that a new generation can look around them and learn to love what they see. You are the man. You must do it.'

It was like a call to arms and I flushed with pleasure as I heard it. Briefly his hand touched my shoulder. He was ready to leave.

'It must sound foolish,' he said. 'Defeat has deepened my faith. And my resolution. Give my regards to Meg. And to Griff when you see him. They are the ones that count. I see them you know like one of those Soviet posters! A young man and a young woman with a flag between them leading the onward march to the promised land.'

He meant it as a humorous comment. All it did for me was close the door on a brief hope of release. I was back incarcerated in the prison of domestic trouble. It was a door that had to be kept closed. Llywelyn and the entire outside world should know nothing of our private anxieties: that was how it had to be, and that was the only measure of comfort available.

I went to the front door to wave them goodbye. The theological student reached under the driving seat of what A.W. called their chariot of fire, extracting the starting handle and waving it cheerfully in the air. He gave a demonstration of his expertise and the engine burst into life. We were after all old comrades. We had fought the good fight and we had lost, and I owed them the affectionate fidelity that remained after such a shared disaster. Behind me inside the house, Olwen was leaning down the banisters at the top of the stairs calling me in an exaggerated whisper.

'Are they gone?'

'Can't you see for yourself?'

Why hadn't they come down in any case? She and Meg. What had they got to complain about? What had they got to hide? They should have presented themselves for some kind of tribute. This man Llywelyn had suffered a grievous defeat and yet his dignified demeanour remained an inspiration to anyone with a modicum of respect for the human spirit.

'Meg is in a state,' Olwen said. 'She's lying on her bed with her knees under her chin and she won't stop sobbing.'

'What nonsense. Losing an election is not the end of the world,' I said.

'It is to her,' Olwen said. 'She says this is a horrid little country. It doesn't stand for anything and it doesn't mean anything. She can't bear to live in it and she refuses to live in it.'

'That's stupid talk,' I said.

'It's not just politics,' Olwen said.

It was absurd that she should speak in irritating stage whispers. Any moment now she would accuse me of never knowing what was going on: of being unwilling to face up to unpalatable facts. When she refrained from doing so the look on her face filled me with foreboding.

ii

A great transfer of power was taking place. Not a Bolshevik upheaval but bad enough. It had touched my shoulder as I was weeding in the neglected garden.

'You can't do that,' he said.

'Can't I? Why can't I?'

As always my instinct was to rebel. If there was a lesson in life I should have learned it was you cannot rebel against a revolution. This man seemed mild enough when he came home from the war. The Lodge was decorated with flags and flowers and "Welcome Home Dad" was printed in large crude letters. Dad was Corporal Melling. A Labour stalwart. And more importantly his cousin was chairman of the Labour-controlled County Council. This Melling was a quiet commissar relying on refurbished Rules and Regulations to assert his power: fire regulations that ladies' rooms should not be locked at night; that keys should be deposited in the caretaker's office; that inspection should take place once a fortnight and that even my personal trowel and fork should be confiscated.

The sun shone and I was able to bend and one of the few pleasures left to me was planting, transplanting, and weeding in the flower beds. It was a way of collaborating with the force of nature and it took me back to the best days of my youth. My maid was enamoured of the second gardener. Those halcyon days.

'That's somebody's job,' the Corporal said. 'We can't have you interfering.'

He was leering down at me with the repulsive self-satisfaction of a man exercising a newly acquired authority. By what right did he tap my shoulder? And why was I struck dumb? I should be saying how much I wanted to help restore these gardens to something approaching their former life. I should protest my desire to contribute my widow's mite towards what they were calling post-war reconstruction.

'In any case you won't be with us much longer.'

He spoke as he moved away exhaling cigarette smoke into the still air. Bad news seemed worse somehow in the sunlight. I felt a pang of attachment to my pleasant prison. It had been my refuge for the last four years. Where would I go? Where would I be sent? There were camps of course for displaced persons. I was the most displaced person in the world.

When I found the strength to move the only direction left to me was the Rectory. Where your treasure is there shall your heart be also. It was an absurd impulse but I longed to deposit my four cartridges with my jewels. Did that dear family realise they might also be threatened with dispossession? That was the way of revolutions. I had my own folk memory of the shock of the Bolshevik upheavals that terrorised my people at the end of the First War. In their innocence they would laugh at me. Provinciality has its charms but a mole-like existence is not conducive to the development of the larger historical perspective. Who else could I talk to? On so beautiful a day to be threatened with lethal isolation.

It was not my preferred route to the Rectory. A path through rocky outcrops, hazelwood, gorse-bushes, bramble patches, over-grown grass and colonies of wild flowers. I used to have a fear of tripping. Today I had already been tripped up and I had nothing to lose. All that was left to me was to make haste and to mutter to myself. Some odd quiver in the back of my neck made me aware of a presence. An animal or a bird disappeared behind the large gorse bush. At some distance on the path ahead of me Meg stood in a pool of sunlight. I called her name. She did not want to hear me. It wasn't me she was waiting for. When I caught up with her she was sitting on an outcrop, her bare legs stretched out on the warm rock and her unsullied peach complexion flushed with anger. On closer inspection the beauty of her face was marred by a petulant frown.

'Meg. What are you doing here?'

I was so helpless myself. Bereft of that guiding power the old should exercise in the affairs of the young.

'I can't bear this place,' she said. 'I really can't. It's nothing but a refuge for the second-rate. That's all it is. I can't for the life of me see what you see in it.'

Of course she could not see herself. The very flower of this forgotten field.

'A country that has lost its purpose has lost its right to exist. That's what's so terrible. It's true.'

I struggled to make my own distress shrink in face of hers. I was old and finished. She was young: had not even started out. What comfort could I bring her. What advice could I give.

'What does your friend say?'

'What friend?'

'Griff Kenyon. Your conscientious objector.'

'He's not mine, for heaven's sake.'

There was nothing the creature longed to be more. And there was no point in saying that. I could see the ray of her displeasure already shifting in my direction. I saw her regret the vehemence of her rejection. She did not mean to disown her Griff.

'I respect Griff. Of course I do. I admire him. But he has his limitations.'

That could only mean one thing. Her life had been invaded, over-run by Klaus Wilhelm Rist. That grinning sewer rat. This was exactly how it should never have been allowed to happen. It was for Rist she was waiting. And was prepared to wait forever. The endless subterfuge of lovers. Her innocence was painful for me to look at. I didn't want her to go through what I had gone through. Is there no way for one generation ever to learn from the mistakes of another?

'They don't want me to see him. That's how it always is. The artist has to fight his way through obstacles. Not to mention huge mountains of indifference. It's always been like that. For the first-rate artist I mean. He's at odds with the forces of inertia. He has to change the direction of an art form before he can contribute to it. These things are so obvious but people can never see them.'

They weren't so obvious to me. These facile bits of casuistry were lessons learnt too rapidly by an infatuated female. There had to be something I could say to put a brake on her headlong descent into folly.

'You think Klaus Rist is a musical genius?'

She resented my presumption in daring to question the fact.

'Of course he is. And he needs me. You can't imagine how difficult it is. His family will want him to go into the business. And my parents ... well. You know what they're like.'

My head was shaking with a sudden deluge of misery. A convulsion beyond my control. The insanity of love was driving her to attack those who loved her most. When she noticed my distress, as is the way with the generous young, her resentment was instantly transformed into sympathy. She would dole out comfort by taking me further into her confidence.

'What am I talking about? It's me that needs him. My life has been changed. I have to admit it. He's given me a glimpse of what it means to be first-rate in every sense. Nothing else will do. You can't put these things into words. I can't anyway.'

I knew what she meant and I bitterly deplored it. She had been sexually roused as she had never been roused before. In the hands of this self-appointed musical genius. He was a soldier that should have been killed while the war lasted. Now he was at large, let loose to do more damage.

'Where is he now?' I said. 'Your musical genius?'

Meg drew back. It was something I should not have said. But what could I say? Some general condemnation of the male of the species? Nothing I could say would be of any use. And what could I do except kill the creature. I had ammunition in my pocket but no gun.

'He's under a terrible strain,' she said. 'He's under so much pressure. That Colonel Bacon is in touch with his family. He wants to send Klaus back because he wants to make business contacts to his own advantage. I'm not blind you know.'

'Meg. My dear. What will you do?'

I should be offering her guidance and advice: not standing there with my mouth open.

'We have our plans,' she said. 'Don't you worry.'

The young. What can you do? They behave as though history had never happened before.

'We know what we're doing. The trick is to keep abreast of the situation and be swift to turn it to your advantage. Speed is everything. Seize the moment.'

That too was her master's voice. The prospect was too awful to contemplate. What would Germany be like next winter? A place of ruins. Famine. Plague. Did she imagine a pair of lovers could take the ruin and rebuild it nearer to their hearts' desire?

Everywhere rubble and rubbish.

'Meg. Listen to me. You have the most loving parents. You must think of them. You must do nothing without consulting them first. Do you hear me?'

She could hear me but she wasn't listening. Klaus Rist had the only voice she could listen to. Just another artiste manqué taking his comfort where he could find it: snatching any compensation for his own inadequacies. If only I could confront the creature. What would ever deter him except the barrel of a gun?

'You know how it is,' Meg said. 'You have to have faith. And you have to trust each other. It's like music Klaus says. Love is like music. It has to win through and triumph in the end.'

iii

Nell Parry was sitting on the stone steps that led to the stable loft where Griff Kenyon insisted on sleeping. It always struck me as one of the penances he imposed on himself: like climbing the wall of the ruined tower to prove he wasn't a coward. The door of the loft was open. The interior looked dark and deserted. Nell had been feeding the hens and the enamelled bowl she nursed in her lap was empty. The whole place was unnervingly quiet. The harvest was over. The cowshed and the outhouses empty with all their doors open. It should have been a picture of peace and plenty: instead it appeared to me like a place under a strange spell. Even the sporadic clucking of the hens was drowsy and muffled.

'He's gone.'

She was talking to herself as much as to me.

'And he won't come back. He will never come back.'

Her voice was brittle and solitary in the stillness of the afternoon. I stood at the bottom of the stone steps to receive her recital of the accomplished fact. Griff was gone and the light had gone out of her narrow life. I knew they thought the world of the lad. Here I was confronted with a love greater than a mother's.

She couldn't have meant it but the drone of her voice was ominous. My head was already tense with a premonition.

'Why did they ever come here anyway. These foreigners. These Germans. Upsetting our way of life. That's what I say. I don't mind work. I never have. He was a good worker, Griff. Conscientious. That's what it means isn't it? I used to listen to them talking. They looked so nice together. They would say things I liked to hear. About the land and so on. They were young of course. They wouldn't know what it was like to feel your bones stiffen. Be afraid of bending in case you never straighten your back again. I told him Rector, as plainly as I'm telling you now. That if he stayed here he could have it all. Inherit. In the fullness of time if not sooner. And Emlyn said it. He wasn't willing but I made him say it. It was no use.'

I was under an obligation to say something. A priest has a special responsibility to justify God's ways to men and men's ways to each other which is just as difficult.

'It's his conscience, Mrs Parry,' I said. 'He's the kind of young man who is compelled to do what he thinks is right. He was always hardest on himself.'

She had no difficulty in agreeing with what I said about Griff. Yet she was gazing down at me with what I could only take to be soulful reproach.

'She wouldn't have him,' she said. 'She wouldn't have him at any price.'

I understood she was taking a poor view of my daughter Meg. This saddened me. Meg had always been so welcome at Hendrefor. How many times when she was growing up did I hear her say how much she loved the place. This was a point I had to make at the first opportunity: Meg loved Hendrefor so much. She idealised it.

'It's not for me to say, but I don't think girls should be allowed to go where they like and do what they like. I don't think so. Where will it end?'

This had to be a not-so-oblique criticism of the way I had brought up my family. Nell Parry was one of my most loyal members. A stalwart of our little congregation. If she was absent her place was conspicuously empty. I could not take umbrage even if I wanted to. The usual course was to diffuse a potential crisis with some bland generalisation.

'The world is changing fast, Mrs Parry. It's hard to keep up with it all.'

'The sacrifice that boy was prepared to make,' she said. 'Offering to marry a girl carrying another man's child. And she refused him.'

It couldn't be true. Just rumour and gossip. I may have been at fault allowing her to run wild around the countryside on that bicycle of hers, but my wife was constantly asserting how wise and responsible our daughter was. And who was I, a mere male, to intervene in an area of feminine understanding that is a special province of mother and daughter. Our father who sits in the study is more than willing to be kept in ignorance. A time comes when such a man has to pay for his comfortable routine of unawareness. The impossible becomes possible. And now I have to listen with rigid attention to what Nell Parry is saying. She sits above me on the stone step like some relentless oracle.

'I told her myself. "You can have this place in the fullness of time," I said. "If that is what Griff wants. He deserves the best," I said. I thought she would want it. All those things they used to say about the importance of the land. The inheritance and so on. All through the election they were still saying it. Like gospel truth. I don't like to say this, Rector. She's your daughter. But it's all her fault.'

And by extension, mine. It had all gone on behind my back. That was no excuse. I chose to keep my back turned. Olwen used to tease me and say that I used history and theology to protect me from reality. This is reality. The seed of a stranger lodged in my daughter's womb. A past irretrievably lost and a future liable to stretch forever out of my grasp.

No more parish visiting. I most urgently needed to go home and confront the crisis on my own hearth. I bicycled with my head down as if the world was watching my discomfiture. I searched the furthest reaches of my memory for all the signs and portents I had so totally failed to recognise. A man is blind if he neglects to look. Why should she lurk outside the door listening to cacophonous music on a damp piano? At what precise moment in time did she transfer her allegiance from Griff to the Prisoner-of-War? The young lead their lives in full view and yet manage to remain out of sight. Surely not during the election campaign. Griff and Meg were so close then and so dedicated. Where was she now? And why had I not confronted her in some way or another long before this? A storm of questions swept through my mind and not one had been answered when I arrived home to find Colonel Bacon's jeep parked boldly within a few feet of my Rectory back door.

There they were, my wife and the Colonel, calmly drinking tea and nibbling biscuits at the kitchen table: the very picture of domestic felicity. He piped up while I was still standing in the doorway.

'Rector! What an instinct! How did you know tea was brewing?'

I lost what little calm I had left.

'Get out of here,' I said. 'And don't come back.'

My own breathing seemed the only form of life in a cold dark silence. The Colonel and Olwen were frozen in the awkward position in which they were caught by my onslaught.

'I say ... I can see you are upset, old chap....'

He was gazing at Olwen as if she existed to provide him with the appropriate cue. My wife was too shocked by the spectacle of my wrath to say anything.

'You are no better than a savage.'

My throat constricted as I pointed at the Colonel, although I knew it wasn't polite to point.

'You have no idea of the sanctity of family life, or of anything else if it comes to that. You are just a barbarian parading about in a uniform....'

I struggled to impose order on my thoughts so that I could heap abuse more lavishly on the man's head. So that I could release the depths of my resentment. Olwen was on her feet at last determined to put a stop to my outburst.

'Edwin! Charles is here to help us.'

I ignored her and raised a threatening hand at the Colonel.

'Clear out!' I said. 'This minute! Do you hear me?'

He tried his best to make a dignified exit.

'Get out of this house!'

Olwen struggled to keep calm: to impose some order.

'Charles. Really. I do apologise.'

The Colonel waved an awkward combination of propitiation and temporary farewell.

'I quite understand. Don't worry. I'll be in touch. I'll do everything I can.'

He was gone and I was left wondering what exactly it was he would do, and what help my wife was expecting from him. She shifted to the window to bid him a final farewell before she turned to give me her attention.

'Did you know that your daughter was pregnant?' I said.

'Yes. I did.'

'By that German Prisoner-of-War your friend the Colonel brought into this house.'

'He wants to help. He is in touch with Klaus's family.'

'Klaus.'

I blurted out the name like a term of abuse. I had to make a greater effort to arrive at a rational discourse.

'Are we supposed to put ourselves at his mercy? Why am I the last to be informed? I mean how much am I expected to put up with. Where is she? Where is the girl?'

Olwen was smiling. I could not understand why my desperation and ill-humour should cause her amusement.

'Fifty-eight Oakley Street,' she said.

'What?'

'Griff is looking after her. They are in a hostel for war-relief workers. In the middle of Chelsea. Griff is joining an unit that is being sent out to China after five weeks intensive training. By then we hope Meg's difficulties will be sorted out.'

'Difficulties. Is that what you call it? And what do we say to people? Why am I the last to be told anything?'

'She didn't want to upset you.'

'Upset me?'

Parrot-like repetitions emphasised my ineffectiveness. I couldn't prevent myself making them.

'And there's Eryl,' I said. 'What are we going to tell Eryl?'

'The truth,' Olwen said. 'What else can you tell a doctor?'

'And the parish? What are we going to tell the parish?'

She gave a deep sigh.

'There you are, you see....'

'See what?'

'That's what worries you most of all. What will people say?'

iv

Between the sprigs of ivy hanging over my window I could watch the festivities in progress in the courtyard. All the inmates were there. Even that pious old ruin Flora Armstrong-Jones. Sterile old women dancing attendance on that tailor's dummy of a Colonel as if they were maidens with ribbons stepping around the maypole tree. The weather is warm enough to permit their own special victory celebrations out of doors, and I can see them buzzing about in the glow of mutual admiration. An occasion to be unstintingly pleased with themselves. What more can old women ask for? Dappled sunlight falls like a benediction on the damask tablecloth. That sinister Corporal and his wife are moving in and out of the shadows asserting their authority through assiduous service. The children have been sent away for the afternoon. I am the only human being left alive in the deserted building: just like a schoolgirl kept in detention for the misdemeanour of unacceptable origins: which is ironic since I am the only authentic aristocrat in the place.

When he arrived I should have gone down and confronted the Colonel. What right had he to parade about and smile and celebrate when I knew he had been instrumental in the ruin of my child? I wanted to face him, accuse him, punish him: and I was afraid to do so because he had the power to order my arrest.

Power flows from the barrel of a gun. It can also trickle from a pen. At two o'clock in the morning I had studied the darkness long enough. Impotence was a living death. At least writing was a form of action. There was my pen and my ever loyal portable Imperial. *I constitute as sole heir to my estate my beloved friend Megan Eluned Pritchard daughter of the Reverend Edwin Henry Pritchard and Olwen his wife…. I exclude from my estate the so-called Nürnberg Cross in the hope that it will find a resting place in the appropriate museum when the new Germany arises from the ashes…. In testimony of which I subscribe my name this night of the twentieth of July in the year nineteen forty five and may God and the scattering of his jewels his constellations witness through the open window my signature my innocence my sanity….* Having written and typed I rested as a soldier does the night before the battle.

There is a logical connection between shooting someone else and shooting yourself. That the war has proved if nothing else. I can take aim through the window. The ivy is my hide and I am a hunter not an assassin. In the old days in the marshes I was complimented on my shooting. More accuracy and less style my Uncle Bunji said when he took the opportunity to squeeze my waist. Not that I minded. He could squeeze my waist and I could squeeze the trigger. All it requires is a bit of nerve.

And a steady hand. I have opened the window and the noise from the courtyard flows in like the twitter of caged birds. The Colonel guest of honour sits at the head of the table. I point the gun at his polished head and a strand of ivy slips across the sights. I have only one pair of hands. I am stiff and infirm but I do not lack resolution. I push myself further through the window. The shotgun will speak in my behalf and execute justice.

That stupid female Letitia Hughes-White has seen the barrel of my gun. She has instantly recognised my intention. Her mouth opens. She jumps up and screams. She upsets my aim. I shoot at nothing and I hit it. The entire flock of females are in motion and screaming at me. What can I do? I can close the window but I can't lock the door. With all my strength I drag my dressing-table in front of it.

This is how dreams come true. How many times in my solitude have I dreamt of being invaded. Now it is happening. Footsteps and voices advance like a rumble of thunder. I lean against the bed exhausted. Am I obliged to shoot myself without the satisfaction of having first shot someone else? That is an inappropriate pattern. I see my dilapidated image in the dressing-table mirror and I loathe what I see. Was it merely for this the whole wretched business of living wore itself out at my expense? At least that mocking likeness I could aim at and destroy. I fired and the face was shattered. The screams outside went on after the splintering explosion. So much noise and panic. As far as I was concerned there was nothing more to be said. The only blood shed trickled into my left eye from a gash made by flying glass.

V

'Strictly speaking she should be in prison.'

Moi bach Melling had become Corporal Melling and had learned to pontificate. I remember how obsequious he used to be. Ignorant, stupid, anxious to please. Not any more. He sat on the edge of the table used for Management Committees smoking a cigarette and raising his arm so that I should notice the chevrons on the sleeve of his battledress. I had spoken in support of A.W. Llywelyn so my cloak of sacerdotal neutrality had been snatched away from me for ever. I was exposed as an object of ridicule and contempt. An entire social spectrum from Tory to Labour, from Sir George Ellis Owen to this promoted servant, could assume the right to regard me as a seditious eccentric, a toothless threat. My political sins were compounded by the antics of a decayed foreign aristocrat and the waywardness of my daughter.

'The fact is, if she were just a working class woman that's exactly where she would be. A breach of the peace.'

In principle it was a good thing that Labour had taken control of the County Council. It was not so good to learn that the Bishop had been discussing the future of this institution with the great Councillor Melling in his capacity as Chairman of one of the numerous sub-committees of the council, without consulting me. This Corporal knew more about what was going on than I did. We used to treat them as a comic turn, Moi and Lizzie Melling. She raucous and obstreperous. He pressing his advantage with an undying eagerness to please. They were no longer funny.

'She should never have been admitted in the first place. The Rules were broken.'

Of course they were. And I broke them. I took the responsibility and now that cousin of Letitia Hughes-White was tramping about the place with copies of minutes sticking out of his coat pocket. That pompous idiot with his gold watch-chain and his spats. The vultures were gathering. Letitia was ill. They claimed she was suffering from shock. Old ladies are mortal and the supply of decayed gentlewomen with the appropriate qualifications is drying up. A transfer of power will take place: painless, unobtrusive, neat, appropriate, seemly. The Church's responsibility would be transferred to the County Council and the Bishop would heave a sigh of relief, and the solicitors, hidden among them Letitia's cousin, would garner the spoils. The fabric of our little society was unravelling before my eyes. At least in war time the buttresses had appeared relatively stable. Now everything was shifting and anything was possible. What little authority I ever possessed was already transformed into fossilised impotence. I could already see the mills of the Melling minds turning: if they played their cards right they could end up owning a profitable private hotel.

'The Colonel asked us not to press charges. So as not to embarrass the Rector he said.'

Was I expected to show gratitude? The vestiges of the respect due to my cloth were dependent on the Colonel's affection for my wife. I squared my shoulders determined to exert what little authority was left to me.

'If you would put the Countess's possessions on a hand-cart, Melling, and bring them over to the Rectory. We'll find room for them above the coach-house for the time being.'

I succeeded in showing sufficient confidence to command obedience. He accompanied me to my car, something of his old manner returning as he dry-washed his hands and ventured to exhibit what he considered diplomatic good will.

'Some of the ladies said the poor woman had some jewel cases hidden in her room. I must say I haven't seen any sign of them.'

He waited for me to speak. I resolved to say nothing. What little I knew was no business of his. And the less he knew, the better. Knowledge, after all, was power.

'She wasn't very popular, as you know.'

It was getting more and more intolerable to have to listen to the fellow.

'I suppose you know that some of the ladies have written to the Bishop to complain about her.... What in the world will become of her?'

He was staring at me through the car window, his sheepdog eyes pleading for any scrap of information I could give him. I resisted an impulse to let him know she had been invited to spend the weekend at Buckingham Palace and drove off.

The jewels were a problem. They should also be a pretext. I needed to talk to the Colonel face to face. I needed a clear view of his intentions and to obtain that I was obliged to apologise for my emotional outburst. If it was his intention to help us with out family difficulties I had to show some gratitude. I would visit the Prisoner-of-War camp like a penitent. Approach the Colonel on my knees. Sacrifice my pride on the altar of my family's well-being. The local paper reported that the authorities were holding back a substantial number of German Prisoners-of-War to help with the corn harvest. This should leave enough time for the essential decencies to be sorted out.

The rows of Nissen huts were laid out just above the marsh

along the estuary. On the headland opposite were Iron Age hut groups. The best preserved had been excavated in the far-away summers of '36 and '37. Why were they so far away? I had a glimpse of Meg aged six or seven running after her big brother always eager to keep up with him. Eryl was so patient and gentle with her: widely recognised as the perfect older brother. As indeed the Rectory family was recognised as a pattern worthy of general emulation. Whatever the shortcomings of the Rector, Olwen was accepted as the perfect parson's wife. Such a pleasant place to picnic in those balmy days. Do they have to be so far away? The harebells still grow on the earthbanks. The dog roses and honeysuckle are still lodged in the hedgerow as though nothing had changed. Rosebay willow herb runs to fluffy seed along the prison fence.

A requisitioned holiday bungalow just outside the camp perimeter was the Colonel's quarters. My approach brought an officer out on to the verandah. A bored young man eager for any form of diversion. I enquired after Colonel Bacon.

'Gone. The lucky old devil. Posted to Helmstedt. A key centre of communications in the British Zone, he said.'

The young man was much concerned to bemoan his own fate. He introduced himself.

'Wenn. Tom Wenn. Two 'ns'. You may as well say I'm left in charge here. Pretty grim really. Missing all the fun. But what can you do?'

He wanted me to sympathise. He was impervious to the beauty of the place. He had no interest in the history. He just sat there nursing his resentment. Even more of an exile than the prisoners he was supposed to be guarding. Another victim of the strange hiatus: the end of one war and the longing to end the other.

'I'm not saying I'm bored out of my mind,' said Major Wenn. 'I know its all over and we've all got to be grateful. I can feel the optimism in the air. I'm jolly pleased with the new government to tell you the truth. A new broom and all that. We've got to sweep clean and make a new start. "Bliss was it in that dawn to be alive" and all that.... Can I offer you some tea?'

He needed someone to listen at length to his complaint. He felt left out. All the action was elsewhere. Parties were in progress and he was not invited. A brave new world was about to be built without his help. I declined his invitation. He tried to understand I had my parish duties to attend to. My routines were only marginally less humdrum and stifling than his. As I turned away he made a last request. It sounded like a forlorn hope.

'Padre. You don't happen to play chess do you? Maybe when you've an hour to spare you could stop by for a game?'

vi

Because I was not included among the mourners I had a distinct impression of witnessing my own funeral. My room at the Rectory overlooked the north side of the graveyard that surrounded the church. I had seen the Rector standing under the lychgate ready to escort me on my last journey. The earth tilted ready to receive me. There was a sympathetic breeze from the south west fluttering his white surplice and he could have been the replica of an earthly angel supervising a tender occasion. His cassock reached to his ankles and made him look thin and ready to float.

Life may or may not be a ceremony but death has to be if any form of civilisation is to continue. In the world I came from the naked dead are being shovelled into mass graves. To lie in state in a silk bed inside a coffin is to be preferred to wandering the scorched streets and scavenging among the ruins. I heard a voice from heaven saying unto me... Blessed are the dead which die in the Lord. My goodness yes. There I shall lie. And there she lies. Letitia Hughes-White. A select group of mourners surround an open grave. She has laid down in her will that she desires a marble headstone and her solicitor cousin or whatever he was grumbles there is not enough money to pay for one. Headstones are messengers between the living and the dead. In life we were at daggers drawn, in death we shall not be divided. My enemy while she lived, my sister now in the graveyard. Now everything shall be made clear and our conversation grow in the silence.

Olwen said there was no delay in emptying her little rooms. Someone turned up with a baker's van and removed the entire contents. Except for the genealogical tree. The glass in the frame had broken and the painstaking fruit of research and calligraphy dumped on the local rubbish heap. Olwen was tempted to rescue it and then decided not to increase the quantity of her encumbrance. She was smiling when she said it and I was not to think that she included me in that category. I had no reason to be sensitive. I was the fortunate recipient of her attentive goodwill. I was quartered in the one place in the whole world I would have chosen. I felt stronger and better than I had felt for years. Even my arthritis seemed to have gone into miraculous recession. Meg is not here but if I am attentive I can hear her voice like music about the silent house. Love operates in absence as well as presence.

A hand presses my arm. Olwen has returned from church. She wears hat and gloves and carries a prayer book. There is a glitter of inexplicable excitement in her eyes. A burial ceremony makes us more aware of the beauty of the earth. Perhaps more at one with its seasons and the magic of their transience. Looking through the window I become attached for all time to this burial place. I shall lie as close as possible to that ninth century wheel cross although I realise that beggars and foreigners cannot be choosers.

'Cecilia. My dear. I have the most awful confession to make.'

I was warmed by the confidence she was showing in me. This dear woman to whom I owe everything. My life had depended on the strength of her character when the whole world had turned against me and I was about to be thrown into prison. How could I ever repay her?

'I'm concerned about Meg. Of course I am. But to tell you the truth she has got more strength of character than I have. She'll come through.'

We had to think that, to comfort each other. A young girl

cannot remain a young girl for ever. I could see her now in the garden in a white summer dress, reading under the apple tree. That transient perfection so capable of uplifting and breaking the heart.

'You mustn't think badly of me. Before I grow old, Cecilia, I want at least a taste of the wicked world.'

The gloves, the hat, the black dress, the prayer-book: a woman I had to make an effort to recognise, let alone understand.

'Just once before it's too late. I don't know how to say it without sounding awful. I just want to escape for a while. It's not that I don't love him, whatever that means. I just want to get away for a while. He may be right and righteous. But if I get away for a while I would become less resentful, I think. What am I trying to say? Making excuses. That's all we do isn't it? Just get away for a while from that daily dose of sententious pessimism.'

She bit her lower lip to stop herself giggling. Then we started to giggle together. The giggle was designed by the devil as a special temptation for women. Or is it a consolation prize? A substitute for the lack of laughing for joy. Whatever it was I would do what Olwen asked. And even then it would be the least I could do.

'It's not an affair,' she said. 'Don't think that for heaven's sake. I don't love him. It's just a case of making use of him. Instead of a man forever making use of me. What's wrong with that? The Four Freedoms. My goodness. The Fifth is even more important. Freedom from male exploitation.'

We giggled even more loudly until we heard the front door bang and were reduced to a conspiratorial whisper.

'I must go to London. There's a place for me with Meg for the time being. Then we shall go to Germany when the Colonel has found a place for us. And then Meg can join her Klaus if she wants to. I shall be able to see the world in a way that I have never seen it before. I shall keep in touch of course. With my Meg and with my Eryl and with here. And you'll be here. And you'll keep an eye on poor Edwin.'

I wanted to restrain her excitement. She was expecting too

much. She had no idea of the awfulness of that world outside she was so eager to visit. I could not bear to think of her relying on that idiotic Colonel and that sly insinuating Klaus Rist. What could I do? These two women that I loved more than anything in the world. All I could do was grasp her hand, shake my head and repeat her name.

'You think I'm being monumentally selfish. Is that what you think?'

'Oh no. My dear. No. No.'

'You are one of the family now, Cecilia. I mean that.'

It was an accolade and I had to smile as I received it.

'It's a bond,' Olwen said. 'We've adopted you. In this place. That's the truth of the matter.'

vii

My son is like me. He never found it easy to express how he feels through talk. He censors his own letters more than he is officially required to. I can sense his hesitations even as I read. He prefers to be cool and clinical and I applaud that. It is the only way to be useful to any community.... *We should be on the move soon. We can't really tell from one day to the next. "Shifting sands" Rees calls it. "You cannot be expected to build on shifting sands." He's not doing too badly. He's managed to get a transfer to an UNRRA Unit as a nutritional officer. Any day now he'll be leaving us. I shall miss him. He's moody and gets very irritable in the heat, but he is humorous and we can talk Welsh together. He's very hot on what he calls "growing roots" these days. "We all need roots" he says, "to try and hold down the shifting sands." And that reminds me. I need a new set of photographs. I lost my wallet last week in the Casbah. Send them as soon as you can. I don't want to forget what my family looks like....*

Hesitations. What am I going to tell him? Your sister is pregnant by a Prisoner-of-War. Your mother is preparing to run off with a fancy Colonel. And your room is now occupied by the Countess von Leiden whom your mother assures me has become part of the family. It is even more difficult to write a letter than to write a sermon.

My fountain pen circles a blank space while I fail to decide what to leave out and what to put in. It would be better if his mother wrote him. She's the one with the explaining to do. She has become glib enough.

Olwen bustles into my study carrying an empty leather attaché case.

'I think this will be just right to carry the jewels. Where have you put the key of the safe?'

All I could do was thump my fist on the desk and shout.

'You are mad. Don't you realise it? Absolutely mad.'

'Now Edwin....'

'Sit down and write to your son. That's what you should be doing.'

'I know exactly what I should be doing. I am taking these jewels to be deposited in the bank vaults used by the Control Commission in London. That's what Cecilia wants. And I am engaging a firm of solicitors on her behalf. And that's how it will be until that von Leiden lot prove their official claim. And that's what Cecilia wants.'

'And that's what your Colonel wants,' I said. 'Do you think I'm blind or something?'

None of the words I wanted to use were available to me. They had taken leave of me just as my wife was taking leave of me. Everything was being taken out of my hands. Out of my control. To be arranged by other people. As for that unspeakable Colonel....

'He's against everything we ever stood for,' I said. 'Can't you see that? "An English Imperialist." Your own words. You said so yourself. An opportunist with his eye to the main chance. An operator. An exploiter. A parasite. You said so.'

'At least he's alive.'

That's what she dared to say as she was packing those accursed jewels into the case.

'And I am supposed to be dead. Is that what you mean?'

'Don't be silly Edwin. I'm doing the best I can for Meg. And for Eryl too.'

'You'll be telling me soon you're doing it all for my sake.'

'In a way I am.'

This was so provocative I wanted to hit her.

'What can you see in him? He's so crass. Treads on everything and everybody. Totally insensitive.'

'He makes me laugh. That's something to be grateful for. I'll make use of him. For all our sakes. People have to make use of each other. You've made use of me for long enough.'

I was so appalled by her cynicism my lips began to tremble. She didn't care how much she hurt me. This wasn't the Olwen I married. This was a callous stranger ready to trample all over my feelings. All she wanted was an excuse to get to her Colonel and to do what she liked. It was something too horrible to contemplate.

'I don't need an excuse, Edwin.'

She had anticipated what I was thinking. She was hauling in power even as I relinquished it. She was robbing me of my manhood and my substance: carrying them away with the jewels in the case.

'You know Cecilia is a more capable creature than you imagine. She's resourceful and loyal. You make use of her. It's what she needs. And thereby do your Christian duty.'

From the door she could see me slump over the letter I was trying to write to my son. And her son. Did she feel nothing for me?

'Edwin,' she said. 'If you want me back you should encourage me to go.'

She spoke with such utter confidence. She expected me to accept her absurd logic.

viii

I don't know where he heard the news. It must have been hanging in the air. I thought news had become something we both preferred not to hear. He had not bothered to recharge the batteries of his old wireless in the study. I was on my knees in front of the kitchen range raking out the cinders. It wasn't exactly a labour of love, but I was the one ordained to do it. He stood in the doorway like a parson with an announcement to make from the pulpit. His mouth took time to open.

'A single bomb has vaporised an entire city in Japan. A single bomb. What will happen to this world?'

He didn't expect me to answer. He stared at me as though I were a scarecrow come to life in order to clear up the ashes under the fire. In church he had this odd habit of hanging his head before he came to an emotional bit: then he would look up at the rafters and shut his eyes tightly as if he were embarrassed by the resonance in his voice. Who put the coal of fire on his tongue?

'Rector,' I said. 'The Bible is quite right. Man-made catastrophes are the worst.'

He looked at me as though he found my comment inane, idiotic. A strange growl emerged from his throat. He turned on his heel and disappeared. For my part I sat in the ashes wishing I hadn't spoken. It had seemed so appropriate, so pertinent. All I had succeeded in doing was breaking a fragile thread of understanding: the mode of living we had established. I had gone to such pains to assure him that in every vicissitude I was on his side prepared to give one hundred per cent support. When he was summoned to the Bishop's palace, I encouraged him to rehearse his defence at the supper table. He disposed of the formal complaints laid against him, one after the other, and I applauded with nods and smiles. His family had not brought the Church into disrepute. On the contrary. His son had been commended and promoted in North Africa. His daughter and his wife were working as unpaid volunteers in a training centre for refugee work. "Volunteers" is an estimable word and I suggested it. I made an effort to keep my eyes open, remain alert and understand such arcane concepts as "Disestablishment" and "Parson's Freehold". It was pleasing to hear the drone of a man's baritone at the dinner table. I was so tired and yet so determined to please. I understood it was the conspicuous role he had played in the election campaign that was particularly frowned upon. Utopian Welsh Christian socialism was condemned on all sides. I had to admit it was an idealistic concept I barely understood. Nevertheless I was greatly relieved it would not cost him his job: all the same pressure could be brought to get him transferred to a less attractive parish.

The threat was beaten off. I understood that when I heard him humming and singing on his way to the bathroom. Someone somewhere had spoken up for him and the cloud of melancholy was lifted. What isolated creatures we are. At least we have the house in common. When I was sure no one was looking I walked around it and blessed the hands that had laid the foundation course of massive boulders on which it was set. Of course I had lived in houses far far larger than this: but they were bodies politic of a by-gone age, maintained by an army of indoor and outdoor servants. This whole place from the kitchen range to the pantry, from the scullery to the wash-house and outhouses, bore the marks of dear Olwen's ordered approach to a labour I struggled to embrace. When Mrs Dee the noisy cleaning woman banged about I escaped as Olwen had done to work in the garden. All I desired was to inherit the habits of her generous spirit.

The long silences of the Rector were at first unnerving. I thought I had learnt to live with them. He had been indulged by his wife and his children. I remember Olwen saying in half-jest that the trouble with Edwin was that he was spoilt by his mother. It could well be true. Perhaps now he was finding it out for himself. I knew from my own experience that we retain a power to transform our own natures all our lives, as long as we do not allow this talent to atrophy. If such power could be exercised at my advanced age there was no reason why it could not operate at his.

I wasn't looking for him, but I found him. In the church I have a special affection for a seat inside the arcades which separate the north aisle from the nave and the chancel. Not exactly a stool of repentance, but it was here that I learned to accommodate myself and my natural impatience to the life I had been ordained to live. In church at least, I used to tell myself, no-one should feel an exile. The time we spent there should repair the weak links between a wayward life and a system of belief. Not that his sermons were a great help. Large tracts of speech wandered in the mist. There was a fragment of fifteenth century glass which let in a soothing coloured light in the morning. At least one could be wrapped in restful silence.

In front of the altar there was a pool of darkness on the polished stone. It was in the shape of a man with outstretched arms. This was our Rector, the Reverend Edwin Pritchard prostrating himself before the altar. It was something he chose to do. Lie flat on the marble floor sending the chill of mortality through his bones. I had found him. I did not wish to disturb him. I did not wish to witness the depth of his despair. In any case what on earth could I say to comfort him?

The house that constituted my refuge must have seemed unbearably empty to him. He had to bear his crisis of the spirit alone. A chattering old woman could not help him. In my bedroom I could play some consoling music for my own benefit on my ancient gramophone. A Mozart sonata, cracks, crackles and all, to cheer me up. On my way upstairs I was struck with a notion that stopped me in my tracks. Perhaps it was the sequence of old prints on the wall that made me think of it. I struck his study door boldly with my stick. To my surprise when I opened the door he was not displeased to see me.

'Rector,' I said. 'Look here. Write your parish history. And I shall type it for you. My fingers are so much better. What do you think? Slowly but surely I shall type it.'

He shook his head, ready to give up already.

'How can you talk of History,' he said. 'Today we have seen the end of it.'

At least he was willing to talk to me. That was better than nothing. He wanted me to sit and listen. In his study he occupied the only comfortable chair. I thought this was to discourage visitors.

'The genie is out of the bottle, Countess. Mankind has found the means to destroy itself. Mankind won't be able to resist the temptation. And I'll tell you why.'

I restrained myself, to allow him to put his case. I was encouraged. If we argue at least we are alive.

'What you have to realise, our fate is in the hands of politicians. Individuals are less than nothing. Can you understand that? And what are politicians? A breed of men who manipulate the lowest instincts of the masses in order to exercise power. Power is their purpose and their pleasure. And our poison. They live to exercise it. We live to suffer. This atomic bomb is the ultimate power. They will never be able to resist using it. Just think of a bankrupt haberdasher playing at being God.'

He was deriving too much satisfaction from his doom-laden pronouncements. Why should he preach at me as if I was sitting in an empty church? Was it all my fault? What he needed was a personality strong enough to disagree with him.

'Rubbish,' I said.

I was ready to risk him taking offence. To my surprise he smiled. I pointed at myself. It was so pleasant to disperse the tension.

'In any case, Rector. I need it.'

'Need what?'

'A parish history. What else am I talking about? We have a right to know all about the place where we live and where we die.'

'This place? This place is not important.'

'It is to me. We all belong to the same world, Rector. I say tomorrow we start.'

About the Author

Emyr Humphreys is the author of twenty novels in English and Welsh, and has also published collections of stories and poetry. He has written screen plays and adapted other works for television and radio, in addition to producing and directing in both of those media. His novels have won the Hawthornden and other prizes.

celebration. Emlyn Parry will be glad to see me. And so will Nell his wife. And I shall enjoy the smell of her giant rice-pudding cooking quietly in the wall oven. The world renews its savour in simple country habits.

Already some of them are drinking oatmeal water in the shadow of the tall hedge. They do not hear me approaching down the grassy lane but I can hear the teasing that can turn to taunting so easily on these occasions. I recognise an adenoidal voice thick with hints and nudges.

'What will you do then, Griff Kenyon? Eh? You've got to do something, good fellow. You can't have a Jerry pinching your best girl. Dammit all. I'm sorry to tell you I've seen them with their arms around each other. Aye. Yes I have. That's what you get, see, for being a conchie....'

A snivelling laugh. Dic Moch mab Meri Ann Clebran — Dick Pig son of Mary Ann Telltale — so what else can you expect? That sly insinuating voice and that wet smile designed to assure every candidate in sight of his vote. I can't see Griff's response. The hedge is too thick. I grip the handlebars of my bicycle, as still as a rabbit mesmerised by a stoat.

'I don't know what her old man would say if he knew. Old man before his time too, if you ask me. Dried up with dry as dust sermons and always clearing his throat. But it's not right, is it? Parson's daughter not supposed to go flirting around the parish. What's the world coming to? It's not a nice thing to see a girl flying around with bare legs on a bicycle.'

No response from Griff. It must be agony and yet he's putting up with it. I admire his restraint. I must get back home and check what that girl has been up to. I keep telling her mother it's time she kept her on a tighter rein. It's up to the mother surely to show her daughter the way. Teach her to exercise the immemorial delicacies of feminine self-control. Lead her along the path a virtuous girl should follow. I have expressed this opinion in one way or another for the last four years and what response do I get? *Meg is a very intelligent girl. She is perfectly capable of looking after herself. I have complete faith in her judgement.* That's what I get.

crow's nest of a pulpit to the sea of empty pews and empty faces.

The haunts of my youth. Home from college. That walk from the station where the late spring merges into early summer and life seemed a promise of perfection. Every lane narrowed by a green expansion of hedges and a familiar world to rediscover. The fields of childhood are unchanged shapes on the slope and the stream below the farm-track is designed to flow on for ever. It still shelters a moorhen and her brood. As you arrive at the narrow crossroads you catch your first breathtaking glimpse of the homestead nestling under the hill. In the field next to the house your brother has already planted potatoes and turnips and the rows are as straight as his back and his pride in his work. And for my birthday as always a boiled egg with my name on it.

The smell of new-mown hay. The fine distinction between mowing the sap-driven grasses of middle June and cutting the hardened stems of mid July. My brother is in charge of a healthy kingdom and I am there to do his bidding. The hay gets heavier as the cart load gets higher and the long days are all work from dawn to dusk. But I never felt freer than when I stood in the empty cart holding the reins and cantering down to the hayfield for yet another load. In those moments I was the master of the little world and the horse in jingling harness my faithful servant. I recall the shock I felt the winter before last when Emlyn Parry spat into the fire and announced the day of the horse was over. He had never liked horses since the day a lumbering Clydesdale had trampled over the corns of his left foot. His pride in his second-hand Fordson tractor showed how willingly he acquiesced in the mechanisation of human existence.

Hard labour. This is what I need. The antidote to the brooding oppression of too much thought. Down at Hendrefor they would welcome my help in the harvest. Off with coat and vest and stiff dog-collar. Roll up sleeves and work until the sweat rolls in rivulets down your back. Harden these soft hands. Never mind bleeding blisters. A farm labourer among farm labourers and Prisoners-of-War, without any function other than contributing his bit to the social harmony that makes the harvest a joyful